William Young

Mathieu Ropars: Et Cetera

Outlook

William Young

Mathieu Ropars: Et Cetera

1. Auflage | ISBN: 978-3-73262-054-8

Erscheinungsort: Frankfurt am Main, Deutschland

Erscheinungsjahr: 2018

Outlook Verlag GmbH, Frankfurt.

William Young

Mathieu Ropars: Et Cetera

Outlook

MATHIEU ROPARS:

ET CETERA.

BY AN EX-EDITOR.

NEW YORK:
G. P. PUTNAM & SON, 661 BROADWAY.
1868.

MATHIEU ROPARS.

From the French of Emile Souvestre.

I.

At the extremity of the roadstead of Brest, in the open space that lies stretched out between the Ile Longue and Point Kelerne, may be seen two rocks crowned with massive granite buildings, and standing boldly up. On the former, the lazaretto of Trébéron has been established; the latter, which in other days was used as a burial-ground and thence took its name of the Ile des Morts, now contains the principal powder-magazine of the naval arsenal. The two rocks separated by an arm of the sea, are about six miles distant from Brest. In appearance these little islands are not unlike. Beyond the ground occupied by the buildings upon them, they offer nothing to the eye save a succession of stony slopes, dotted here and there with coarse moss and prickly thorn-broom. Vainly there might you look for any other shelter than that afforded by the fissures of the rocks, for any other shade than that of the walls, for any other walk than the short terrace contrived in front of the buildings. Naked and sterile, the two isles remind you of a couple of immense sentry-boxes in stone, placed there for the purpose of keeping guard over the sea, which is roaring beneath them. But if the foot that treads them remains imprisoned within a narrow circle, the view from their summit extends over an infinite space. Here, you have the bay of Lanvoc, bordered by a dull- looking and stunted vegetation; there, Roscanvel with its shadows crossed by the graceful spire of its church; there, Spanish Point bristling with batteries; and lastly, close upon the horizon lies Brest, with its dock-yards, its forts, and the hundred masts of its ships, visible through a veil of mist. Midway opens out the Goulet, the harbour of this marvellous lake, through which arrive and depart unceasingly those wandering sails, that issue forth to flaunt the ensign of France upon the waters, or to bring it home again from far-away lands.

A cannon-shot, the echo of which was still booming along the shores, had just announced one of these arrivals, and a frigate, with a light breeze, was doubling the Point under a cloud of canvas. From the esplanade of Trébéron a man, wrapped in a pilot-cloth cape and wearing a narrow-brimmed glazed hat, under which it might be seen that his locks were turning grey, was looking at the noble vessel as she glided along in the distance, between the azure of the sea and of the sky. It was obvious that the keeper of the lazaretto (for he it was) gave but casual attention to the sight, with which his long residence at Trébéron had familiarized him. His look, for a moment resting carelessly upon the frigate which had begun to brail up her upper sails, soon reverted to his more immediate neighbourhood, and settled itself at the foot of the pathway, that led from the esplanade to the sea, upon a group which appeared more decidedly to interest him. And in truth the object of this rivetted gaze was of that sort which might have attracted the least attentive eye. A pupil of Phidias would have traced in it the germ of one of those antique bas-reliefs, of which the marble has become more precious than gold.

Two little girls and a goat were coming up the winding path together. The elder of the two, who might be eleven years old, was holding the freakish animal by one of those long pieces of sea-weed that resemble strips of Spanish leather. Her black hair fell down upon a neck embrowned like a raven's wing, and threw something of a wild hardihood into her expression, tempered however by the velvety softness of her eye. The younger, seated on the goat as though it were her customary place, was of such rosy-white complexion as you see in the flower of the eglantine. A tuft of broom, mingling with her golden hair, fell down upon her shoulder, and gave her an indescribably coquettish grace. The two sisters compelled the goat, which submitted most unwillingly, to moderate its pace; but still, as they proceeded, they were obliged to double the slender reins by which they kept it within bounds, and anon to catch hold of the wreath of sea-flowers twisted about its horns. Then what joyous shouts and peals of laughter were there without end, broken in upon by the gentle bleatings of *Brunette* as she pawed the ground with her foot, and shook her saucy little head! Any other hands but those of Josèphe and Francine would have tried in vain to make her even so far submissive; but for the latter the goat had been a foster-mother, a circumstance evidently not forgotten.

Mathieu Ropars had been watching for some time this pleasant little contest between the fantastic *Brunette* and his daughters, when he felt a hand laid upon his arm; he turned round and encountered, so to say, close against his shoulder the bronzed and smiling face of their mother.

—"Just look at those children," said he, nodding his head in the direction of the merry group.

—"Heavens! Francine will fall," exclaimed the mother, stepping towards the path. He drew her back.

—"Let them be," said he; "don't you know that there is nothing to fear when Josèphe has her eye upon them? Besides, *Brunette* loves them better than her own kids; nor are they behind-hand in returning it. Heaven forgive me, if that creature isn't what they think most of—after us!"

—"And after Monsieur Gabriel," chimed in their mother—"at least so far as Josèphe is concerned; for although he scarcely stayed more than a week in the lazaretto, and that's three years ago, the child never lets a day pass by without speaking of him."

—"To tell the truth, the Lieutenant is a sort of man not easily to be forgotten," replied Ropars, "especially by the little one yonder, to whom he was so kind and made so many promises. Why, wasn't he to bring her all manner of wonderful things from the East? And by the bye, if nothing has happened to him, I believe that we shall pretty soon see him again, as well as the *Thetis*."

—"In the meantime I must tell the children of another visit, which will also be no small treat for them."

—"Whose?"

—"Cousin's, and little Michael's."

—"Dorot's coming?" inquired Mathieu, looking towards the platform of the Ile des Morts. "How do you know?"

—"Can't we talk by signal just as well as his Majesty's ships?" said Geneviève laughing. "Look, he has hung out of his window three small red handkerchiefs; that's to tell us that he's coming over. Besides, I saw Michael going down to the Superintendent's."

—"Bravo!" cried Ropars, his face lighting up; "your cousin and the boy must sup with us—that is to say, if your pantry is not quite so empty as your hospital."

Geneviève protested, and then enumerated with an air of complacency all her culinary resources, which had fortunately been replenished, two days before, by the Superintendent, who supplied at the same time the powder-magazine and the lazaretto. Mathieu promised to complete the feast by broaching for the artillery-man an old bottle of Rousillon wine, stowed away for a long time under the sand of his cellar.

The two little girls at this moment came up on to the terrace.

—"Quick, here!" cried Geneviève, "quick; there's somebody coming."

—"Monsieur Gabriel?" asked Josèphe, springing forward with this exclamation.

—"No, no, goose-cap—cousin Dorot and little Michael."

An involuntary gesture of disappointment escaped from the child; but Francine clapped her hands and broke out into shouts of joy. The goat, left to herself, bounded along the precipitous slopes of the rocks, where she set to work browsing on the tufts of brackish herbage; the sisters took each other's hand to go down towards the little landing-place; whilst their mother went into the house with a view of getting everything in readiness.

As had been remarked by the last-named, the special affection of Josèphe for Monsieur Gabriel was already of several years standing. It dated from a quarantine performed at Trébéron by the Lieutenant, who, charmed by her grace, bordering though it was upon the savage, had exhibited towards her a marked regard, to which the child had responded with what amounted almost to a passion. Having entered the navy against his inclination, Monsieur Gabriel had adopted little of it but its uniform. In the midst of a life of change, hardship, and adventure, he dreamed unceasingly of the unchangeableness of the domestic hearth, and of peaceful family enjoyments. He was one of those lovers of solitude, who are born to live amongst labourers, and women, and children. Confined to the lazaretto of Trébéron, he had brought thither a few favourite books, and his violin, on which he played for hours at a time, with no other end than the listening to its melodious vibrations. When he went out, Josèphe ran to meet him, acted as his guide along the rocks, and escorted him to their most secluded recesses, in which, day by day, he discovered some unknown plant, or moss that was new to him. In the evening, be paid a visit to the old quarter-master whose quiet enjoyment of life had attracted his notice. Geneviève talked to him of her children; Josèphe begged of him a story or a song; and when it was time for him to retire for the night, he went back to his cell, light hearted and with tranquil mind. A fortnight thus slipped away as if it had been an hour; so that when his quarantine was at length performed, and it was necessary for him to leave Trébéron, his deliverance did but awaken in him a feeling of regret. He came back several times to pass whole days upon the lonely islet; and when finally he was embarking for a distant voyage of discovery, he promised the solitary family that he would occasionally write to them. Ropars had in fact received some letters from him; and, as we have seen, was expecting his speedy return. For the moment, the visit announced by Geneviève exclusively occupied the keeper of the lazaretto. He remained alone upon the esplanade, whence he continued to look towards the Ile des Morts. The distance rendered visible everything done there; it was easy to recognize persons and to distinguish their movements. He could therefore see Dorot take his way towards the skiff, set up the mast, and hoist the sail; and the little Michael catching hold, with some difficulty, of the tiller.

Previously to the two families becoming allied by marriage, the keepers of the powder-magazine and of the lazaretto had known each other in the navy, wherein one was a quarter-master and the other a sergeant of artillery. Appointed to Trébéron, Mathieu Ropars had rejoiced at the idea of meeting his old ship-mate Dorot, already several years established at the Ile des Morts, with his wife, his son, and a female orphan relative. The lazaretto being almost always deserted, he was left with ample leisure for frequent visits to the powder-magazine, and for becoming well known there and thoroughly appreciated. Geneviève, Dorot's cousin, was particularly taken with such a character, so straight-forward and yet so gentle. She had been tried, until she was sixteen, by all the pains and penalties of misery. Taken then, from charitable motives, into the house of her cousin whose wife occasionally made her pay dearly enough for his hospitality, the poor orphan had accustomed herself to expecting nothing at any one's hands, and to receiving as a favour whatever was accorded her. Thus the frank cordiality of Mathieu was more touching in her eyes than it would have been in those of another. She welcomed it with a gratitude half filial, to which insensibly became added that shade of a more tender feeling, always blended into the attachments of a woman whose heart is disengaged. An intimacy between herself and Ropars went on, strengthening from day to day, whilst neither of them took account of their predilections. As he marked the young girl in the bloom of her expanding beauty, Mathieu, who already felt the weight of years upon him, would never have dreamed of asking her to share his existence; whilst Geneviève, happy in seeing him daily and in the consciousness of his immediate neighbourhood, thought not of desiring anything further. It needed the offer of a situation for her at Brest, and the consequent prospect of a separation, to enlighten them as to their mutual dependence on each other. Perceiving that Geneviève shed tears, Ropars, who could not shut his eyes to his own distress of mind, took courage and brought matters to a point. He told her that she might dispense with this separation, if the isle of Trébéron were no more irksome to her than the Ile des Morts, and if his society were as agreeable to her as that of her cousin. The poor girl, weeping, blushing and overjoyed, could only reply by letting herself fall into his arms. The old quarter-master forthwith opened his mind to Dorot. The marriage took place; and he carried off Geneviève to his islet, of which henceforth he mistrusted not the solitude.

The difference in their respective ages did not seem to mar the happiness of the keeper and the orphan girl. Both were possessed of that which renders marriage a blessing—the simple mind and the heart of kindly impulse. Children came, to draw still closer these ties, and to enliven their hearth. The younger was just born, when Dorot lost his wife, and was left alone with his son Michael, thirteen years of age. This premature widowerhood had revived the friendship of the two old shipmates. Their intercourse became more frequent. The skiff that served both establishments was stationed at the little haven of the Ile des Morts, and was thus at the disposition of the artillery-man, who missed no opportunity of coming to pass a few hours with his neighbours. But notwithstanding their proximity, and the ease with which the passage was made, these visits could not be of daily occurrence. Dorot was obliged to be constantly on the watch; his official orders were equally sudden and unforeseen; nor could he expose himself to the risk of too frequent absence. His appearance therefore at the lazaretto had not ceased to be a happy exception to the rule. Father, mother, and children alike found in it a festal occasion; and it was never without great rejoicing that the signal was observed announcing the agreeable visit, and the boat seen putting out from the little landing-place and stretching over towards Trébéron.

This time, so soon as Ropars saw her on the way, he went down to meet her. Scarcely had she touched the ground, when Michael jumped ashore, threw his arms about the keeper, then about the two little girls, and then ran off with the latter towards the house. Dorot stepping out in turn, shook hands heartily with Mathieu; and the pair, chatting, slowly began the ascent. Having reached the summit of the cliff, they faced about by force of habit, to take a look out to sea. The artillery-man remarked that the frigate had just clewed up her lower sails.

—"God help us! she's going to anchor," said he; "did you ever see, Mathieu, a homeward-bound ship let go so far from land?"

—"That depends," replied the old quarter-master; "we hold off when we mistrust a fort, or are afraid of reefs."

—"But there's nothing of that sort here," remarked Dorot; "the frigate has no need to fear the guns of the Castle which are her very good friends, or the roadstead which is as safe an anchorage as if she were fast in the dry-dock. There must be something extraordinary."

—"Perhaps the ship has to perform quarantine," suggested Ropars; "the *Thetis* is expected."

—"That's it; you've named her," cried the artillery-man, winking his eye and shading his forehead with one hand so as to look more fixedly at the distant vessel; "it is the *Thetis*, or I'm a heathen. I had her down yonder for a week, when she took her powder on board; I know her by the set of her masts and by her bearing on the water."

—"The *Thetis*!" echoed Mathieu; "then we shall soon see Monsieur Gabriel. What delight for Josèphe! Quick; let's tell her."

He was hurrying off, but Dorot kept him back. "No hurry," said he; "never reckon too surely on what a ship brings home. Pick people out, and they're just those that are missing when the roll's called. Better wait till the

Lieutenant brings his own news."

—"You're right," replied the quarter-master; "the more so since the frigate comes, if I don't mistake, from the Havannah."

—"Who knows whether she won't bring you some lodgers for your lazaretto?"

—"So be it; they'll be welcome. With Geneviève and the children, one can't be dull; but once in a while there's no harm in a little company. You fellows at the Ile des Morts, you have the artillery despatch-carrier, who keeps you up to all that goes on, to say nothing of inspections and your convoys of powder; whilst here—never a thing! Not one visitor in a twelvemonth! At least, if you have to put people sometimes into quarantine, you hear what's done on land there, and that leaves you some thing to talk about for months."

The artillery-man shrugged his shoulders—"That's all very well, when they don't bring disease with them; but the old coasters still talk of a quarantine in which the lazaretto ran short of both earth and rock for burying the dead, and when the bodies were of necessity thrown into the sea with a shot attached to their necks, as in vessels out on a voyage."

—"Now may Christ spare us such a trial!" exclaimed Ropars, respectfully touching his hat, as he was used to do whenever he pronounced the Saviour's name. "But you're speaking of a long time ago, Dorot; please Heaven, we won't see such again. There are no heathen here now; and I believe that God's good will will take care of us."

Dorot nodded his acquiescence. In fact this confidence, springing from a simple faith, had up to that time been justified by experience. During the thirteen years that the keeper had spent at Trébéron, he had only received healthy persons into quarantine, who were complying with a formal regulation, and were obliged to make proof of their good health by undergoing this preventive sequestration. There were indeed rare exceptions. Like all lazarettos, that of Trébéron remained generally unoccupied; and the keeper kept watch there alone, like an ever-living sentinel posted in advance of the continent, for the purpose of warding off contagion.

As they chatted, Dorot and he had reached the house. Geneviève was waiting for them at the doorway, surrounded by the three children who laid hold of and talked to her all at once. After an exchange of their accustomed friendly greetings, she went in, with the two keepers, whilst Michael drew off Francine and Josèphe towards *Brunette*, who was waiting for them on a pinnacle of rock, eyeing them and bleating at them. The youngster, accustomed to chase his father's sheep upon the declivities of the Ile des Morts, endeavored to get at her; but the capricious creature sprung from point to point along the precipices, letting herself at every moment almost be caught, and at every moment bounding away from the hand that just could touch her.

Whilst the children kept up this chase, with a thousand calls to one another and a thousand peals of laughter, Ropars and Dorot entered the eating-room in which Geneviève was already laying the cloth. It was a room of middling size, furnished by the keeper himself at the period of his marriage, and ornamented with a few marine engravings. Amongst these was particularly distinguished a portrait of Jean Bart, that nautical Hercules on whom, as all the world knows, his traditional celebrity has fastened all manner of superhuman exploits and impossible adventures.

Having made his guest sit down, Mathieu went off to disinter his bottle of Rousillon wine; and brought it back all whitened with the sand, and capped with a green-waxed cork that bespoke its noble birth-place. Dorot good-temperedly complained of such extravagance, and hinted that he could not make his visit a long one, inasmuch as the officer commanding the post of the Ile des Morts had charged him to bring the skiff back before sunset. Geneviève therefore hurried herself to serve up the dinner, and called the children to take their places at table.

With persons whose entire life was contracted within the narrow limits of two small islands, the conversation could not be much varied. Mathieu talked of his still-lines set between the headlands of Trébéron, and Dorot of his small cherry-tree. The latter might be regarded as the one stumbling block of pride, over which the habitual modesty of the worthy sergeant was sure to trip. No other keeper before his time had succeeded in securing what he planted, from the sea wind; this was the only tree that had ever been seen in the two islands; and Lucullus might well have been less proud of the first cherry-tree that he brought from Persia, for the purpose of gracing his triumph. Humble as regards everything else, Dorot drew himself up proudly when there was any question of his poor wild-stock; he only let it be seen by his friends and his superiors, and then at their urgent solicitation. Objects resemble human kind, and very often assume the importance that is given them, in place of that to which they are entitled. Thus overcharged and carefully tended, the fame of the cherry-tree of the Ile des Morts went abroad from Plougastel to Camaret; it was everywhere talked of as a prodigy. The pride of Dorot had increased in a corresponding degree, and was just now swollen to the highest pitch by an event no less extraordinary than unforseen. He brought the news of it to Trébéron, but would not make it known too abruptly. All supposable things were first to be run over, as in the famous letter of Madame de Sevigné on the marriage of Mademoiselle. Finally, when every one had given it up, he determined to enlighten them, and announced … that the cherry-tree was in blossom!

Unanimous was the cry of astonishment and delight. Prisoners in their island, it was several years since Ropars and Geneviève had seen a tree in blossom; and the two little girls could not recall to mind that they had ever seen one. Loudly and both at once, they beset Michael with questions. Was the cherry-tree flowering in gold-colour like the thorn-broom, or in the colour of blood like the sea-furze? How could the blossoms ever become fruit? Must they wait a long time? Would the tree bear the red cherries of the coast, or the black-hearts of the upper country? Dorot cut all these inquiries short, by declaring that he would come over next day, for the whole of the family, that they might see the wondrous tree and dine at the Ile des Morts. The ecstacies of the sisters may be imagined. Their mother could not check their laughing and their clapping of hands. They continued their cry of "to-morrow, to- morrow!" just as Æneas' look-out men kept up their cry of "Italy, Italy!" when they saw through the empurpled vapours that goal of so many efforts and such longings.

Remarking their impatience, the sergeant proposed to carry them over, that very evening, with Michael. There would be still day-light enough on their arrival, for them to see the cherry-tree covered with its coat of summer-snow, and their parents could fetch them, next day. The children backed this offer with their entreaties; Ropars smiled, without replying; but Geneviève entered her protest against it. What would she do, if Francine and Josèphe were away? Many a time ere this, on waking in the middle of the night, she had fretted herself at not hearing their gentle breathings; she had jumped up in agony, and had crept on tip-toe to their bed, to touch them and to listen to them; how would it be then, if they were not there; how could she herself sleep quietly without fancying some danger? She would dream that the powder-magazine was on fire, or that the Ile des Morts was going down like a vessel foundering
—and all this was said betwixt a laugh and a tear. The little maidens, bent at first on setting off, were soon hanging on their mother's shoulders, touched by her contagious tenderness, and declaring that they preferred to remain. The artillery-man insisted no longer. He took with Mathieu the path that led down to the sandy shore, and was followed by Geneviève and the children, all silent for the moment.

The sun declining to the horizon lit up the promontory of Kelerne, and painted in the passage of Goulet a stream of purple and gold. A breeze began to play over the bay, and chequered it with undulating ripples. The perfume exhaled from the saps was wafted in puffs of wind from the main land, as were the tinklings of the Angelus, and the lowing of the cattle driven home. A consciousness of strength in repose was perceivable, together with an indescribable air of serenity, that stole from surrounding objects upon the senses, and found its way to the very depths of the soul. The sky, the earth, and the water seemed by mutual consent to have subdued their voices, in order to mingle them in one harmonious murmur. Without analyzing the soft but not enervating influence that surrounded them, the two keepers with their families were alive to its effects. Silently they went down the foot-path, pausing upon their steps, as though to lengthen out the sense of enjoyment, or to taste of it drop by drop. Having, however, reached the boat, it became necessary to part. Josèphe made the sergeant promise to come for them early in the morning. The sail at last was hoisted; and the skiff, launched out upon the yielding waves, sped her way towards the powder-magazine.

At the moment when she reached the middle of the channel that separates the two islands, a ship's long-boat, unobserved hitherto in the excitement of leave-taking, appeared to leeward of Trébéron. Her peculiar build, her black color traversed only by a single white ribbon at the water-line, and the perfect condition of her spars and sails, would have sufficed to show what she was, even if the costume of the double row of sailors ranged along the thwarts had not betrayed the man-of-war's men. On crossing the skiff steered by the sergeant, she was sheered suddenly off; and by the last glimpse of day-light might be discerned the yellow flag of the Health Office.

At this sight, Geneviève and the children uttered an involuntary cry. All three at once comprehended that these were occupants coming to the lazaretto; that they would put the island into quarantine, and prevent all external intercourse. The next day's visit must be indefinitely postponed, and the cherry-tree would have finished blossoming before they could have regained their liberty. This dashing down of a newly-raised anticipation had in it something so abrupt and so unexpected, that Francine and Josèphe could by no means resign themselves to it. Desolate was the look that they exchanged, and silently did they begin to weep, as their mother took one of them in either hand, and sorrowfully remounted the path. Geneviève herself felt her heart oppressed; on reaching the platform, she could not but pause for a moment. The skiff with rose-coloured sail, that bore away the promise of another meeting and of a festival, had disappeared; the black long-boat was there at her feet—and with it had come to shore, seclusion, melancholy, and disease. Geneviève kissed her children; but scarcely could she keep back a tear that had gathered beneath her eyelids, as without the inclination to prolong her look she hastily entered the house.

Mathieu in the meantime had gone to receive the persons placed in quarantine, and to open the lazaretto for them. On returning, he looked somewhat pale, and his face wore an expression with which Geneviève was struck; but at the first question she asked him, he abruptly interrupted her, to inquire where Francine and Josèphe were.

—"Don't you see them?" she replied, pointing to the two little girls sitting down in a dark corner, still sobbing, and with eyes still moist; "did you think that they had gone with their cousin?"

"Would to God, they had!" murmured Mathieu in an agonized voice, but not overheard by the children.

Geneviève looked at him, stupefied. "Why so?" she asked; "what has happened? Tell me, Mathieu, in the name of the Holy Trinity! what is the matter?"

—"Well, then," answered the keeper, "there is ... there is ... death upon the island."

—"How do you mean?"

—"I mean, my poor wife, just what I have seen! The *Thetis's* long-boat has landed her hospital-mates and doctors, with eight sick men; not one of whom will ever touch the main-land again."

—"Holy Virgin! what is it?"

—"The yellow fever!"

II.

For him who dwells in-land, the yellow fever is but a disease similar to a thousand others, of which he knows nothing save the name. Family tradition and personal experience can attach to it, for him, neither terror or regret. But amongst our maritime population, the word sounds like a knell; not only bringing to mind a risk to be encountered, but reviving affliction, of recent or of ancient date. There, where every family has one at least of its loved members absent in foreign countries, the terrible scourge is all too well identified with the number of widows and orphans that it has made. It ranks with the storm and the reef of rocks, as a deadly foe. Its name, let fall, produces the same effect as the wind that whistles, or the surf that roars. Looks are interchanged on hearing it; and thought recurs to the absent, if not to the dead.

Ropars, on this occasion, dwelt mainly on those about him; and in truth, no one could have better right than he to be ill at ease. Thrown in former days upon a station where the yellow fever was epidemic, he had seen the seamen of the fleet decimated around him, and had himself barely escaped, as if by miracle. The remembrance of that butchery, as he termed it, was too vivid, and he had too often described it to Geneviève, for their firmness not now to be shaken. They troubled not themselves on their own account, but on account of those whose existence was so dear to them. Mathieu's first thought was of his wife and of his children; the first impulse of Geneviève was to fold them in her arms, and to declare that they must all go away. Some trouble had the old sailor in making her comprehend that, even if retreating were not dishonorable for him, it had become impossible. The long-boat had made sail for the frigate, and the yellow flag was hoisted at the lazaretto. Quarantine had begun for all who happened to be at Tréberon. Not a soul could henceforth pass beyond its limits: and Ropars pointed out to Geneviève the gun-boat sent by the health officer, which had been brought to bear at half cable's-length distance from the island, and cut off from it all intercourse by boats. They were in fact definitively penned in with the epidemic, and condemned to run its risk to the end.

But the agitation of Mathieu, in which surprise had worked its part, did not last long. The quarter-master soon regained his original strength of mind, which had been slightly unhinged in the tendernesses of his domestic life; and, regardless of his own previous words, he set himself seriously to soothing the terror of Geneviève by underrating the danger that they incurred. After all, they were not here in a state of things that favoured the disease; they had not to contend against the enervating sun of the Havannah or Brazil; this was not one of those awful contagions that spread from house to house like a fire, leaving behind it the dead alone—it was a disorder partly spent, and from which, with certain precautions, escape was easy. The chief and the most indispensable of these precautions was to avoid going near the apartments occupied by those who had been brought into quarantine, and never to stay to leeward of the lazaretto. Josèphe and Francine were at once informed of this. Geneviève explained to them every thing that they were to do, with a minuteness of detail, that savoured alternately of threatening and of endearment. At first, as the punishment for any failure of obedience, she pointed out to them the disease, or even death itself; then seeing them turn pale with fear, she drew them within her caressing arms and re-assured them by her kisses. Mathieu added to her exhortations something more definite and more secure. Next morning, he marked out a space enclosed with stakes joined together by a cord, as the children's permitted bounds. By way of increased precaution, the goat herself was brought within this enclosure, picketted to a stake, and fed upon winter fodder. The keeper, on his part, held aloof from habitual intercourse with the infirmary-men and the doctors of the lazaretto He would even have been ignorant of the fate of those who were in quarantine if, every evening, the descent of a few men towards the sandy shore of the little isle, and the tinkling of a bell that warned him to stand out of their way, had not made it obvious that their errand was to dig a grave. The vacancies, besides, were rapidly filled by fresh invalids brought on shore by the frigate's long-boat, for the epidemic did not seem as yet to decrease or to relax its severity. No convalescent inmate had yet appeared upon the terrace of the lazaretto. The skiff belonging to the gun-boat, that enforced the sanitary regulations, came near the landing place every morning; but no one landed. Provisions and medicines were put ashore by means of a travelling pass-rope, set up in the creek; the Surgeon's report was received at the end of a boat-hook; and then the skiff sailed away in an apparent hurry, that bespoke the fear of contagion.

However, after the first few days were past, Ropars and Geneviève felt somewhat re-assured. The blows that death dealt around them were mute and hidden; the edge of inquietude became insensibly blunted. Seeing that it was possible to live in contact with the formidable malady, they half forgot, both of them, that is was also possible to die. It was with them as with the inhabitants of a besieged city, who no longer tremble at the roar of cannon. In vain did the bell tinkle every evening, and the long-boat bring ashore every morning a fresh batch of the death-stricken; the continuance of the danger made it seem to be a matter of course, and this feeling soon merged into a sense of security. Once in a while even, Geneviève forgot every thing and recommenced her singing; but abruptly it was suspended at sight of the yellow flag, or as a sudden recollection crossed her mind. Then the song was stifled into a sigh.

Ropars had made inquiries for Monsieur Gabriel, on the first arrival of the sick. The epidemic had not then attacked him; but his own breaking off from all intercourse with the hospital-mates, and with the crew, had prevented his seeking further information. Several boat-loads had been brought ashore, without any opportunity for his hearing of the Lieutenant, when he received a note, cut through with scissors and steeped in vinegar. It contained only these few words, written in pencil:

"I am come here…. If I live, we shall meet…. If I die … present this letter to the captain of the *Thetis* … and claim for Josèphe … my large mahogany chest.

GABRIEL."

The writing, scarcely legible, betrayed a hand that shook with fever. Mathieu, grievously taken by surprise, forgot this time all his precautions, and ran to the lazaretto. But the Surgeon would not let him see the Lieutenant, whose condition seemed to give him grave concern. In the evening it was still worse, and left little room for hope; on the following day there was none at all.

Josèphe, from whom they had concealed the name of the frigate that was ravaged by the epidemic, had no suspicion of the danger of her friend; still, her sister and herself had none the less lost all their gaiety. Prisoners within the narrow bounds marked out by their father, they were both moodily seated near the stake to which the goat was picketted; and she, lying down at their feet, seemed to disdain the fodder that was scattered before her. Josèphe, holding Francine propped against her, proposed to her, one after another, all the little games to which they were accustomed; but the child shook her head, her eyes fixed upon the sea.

—"What will you do, then, Zine?" asked she, saddened by her sister's sadness.

There was no reply. The elder had one hand upon the younger's head, and played for an instant with the ringlets of her golden hair.

—"You're longing to go across there to see Michael? isn't that it?" she resumed, bending down over the little one; "but it's too late; the cherry-tree has shed its blossoms."

—"Then you believe that the cherries are already ripe?" interrupted Francine, turning up to Josèphe her face that listlessness had robbed of a portion of its roses, but with her large eyes full of curiosity.

—"I don't know," said the elder "mother will tell us. But let's think about something else; you know that we cannot go to the powder-magazine."

—"No, nor to the end of the island, nor any where," added Francine, letting herself sink down again upon Josèphe's knees.

The latter, bent at all events on amusing the child, then called her attention to the goat, that had just got up. Starting suddenly from her doze, *Brunette* was describing round her stake a series of such droll evolutions, that the child's sadness could not hold out against them, and she soon broke out into a laugh. Josèphe, who at first had chimed in with her merriment, was afraid that the mutinous creature's gambols would end by her breaking the cord; she put her hand out to prevent it.

—"Let her be, let her be!" cried Francine in high glee; "look how she rears up! see how she dances! Well done, *Brunette*; higher, little one, higher!"

The child, kneeling down upon the sand, clapped her hands, with shouts of delight; and the goat, that seemed excited by her voice and by the noise, redoubled its capricious boundings. All at once, the stake, loosened by such continued tuggings, was drawn out of the ground: the animal jumped to one side; and finding itself no longer held back, started off for the further extremity of the island.

The two sisters gave utterance to a cry, and then, from an irresistible impulse, sprang away together in pursuit. The corded limits were passed, and they were soon led off along the declivities, calling to *Brunette*, who according to her old tricks would wait, bleating, for them, and then caper away at their approach. In the eagerness of their chase they thus reached the summit of the island, followed the slopes that went down to the sea, and finally arrived at the foot of the ravine that was farthest removed from their dwelling. It was there only that Josèphe bethought her of their disobedience. She stopped, out of breath, and held back her sister with her arms.

—"Not a step further, Zine!" cried she; "we ought not to have come so far; mother forbid it."

The little one looked round about her, and remarked in turn the spot in which they were. It was a large fissure hollowed out in the stony soil of the island, and, at the bottom of which broad ferns and flowering brooms had sprung up in tufts. Right and left, through the partition-walls of rock, peeped up the stonebreak, and the sea turf with its purple cats-tails, and the fox glove that thrust its long stalk from the crevices, loaded with rose-coloured bell flowers.

At such a sight, Francine could not restrain a cry of admiration. Here was the first verdure, here were the first flowers she had seen, since strict orders had confined her to the barren platform occupied by the keeper's house. Neither could she resist the temptation; slipping away from the hands of her sister, and unwilling to hear a word, she disappeared in the thickest of the flowering tufts.

Having vainly called to her, Josèphe followed to bring her back; but the child went on from shrub to shrub, without any inclination to stop. At every fresh handful of gathered flowers, uselessly did Josèphe cry, "enough!" "More, more!" was Francine's answer, as she piled up within her apron, upheld by the two corners, all on which she could lay her hands. Want of place alone could make her consent to suspend her harvesting. Loaded with herbs and wild flowers, falling in garlands down to her very feet, she at length was disposed to take hold again of Josèphe's hand, who set to work to find their way back, and cautiously removed the prickly-broom from their path.

The children were on the point of reaching a ridge made up of heath and broom, when the warning bell was heard above their heads. They stopped, and raised their eyes. Four of the infirmary-men were coming down towards the ravine, bearing their funereal burden. They were following the only foot- path practicable on the slope, and the little girls could not proceed on their way, without meeting them. Terrified, they drew back amongst the bushes that still concealed them, and paused, leaning one against the other. The bell tinkled by fits and starts, drawing nearer at every sound. At length they could distinguish the heavy footstep of the bearers ringing upon the rock, and could see their darkening outlines marked out in the twilight. They were advancing precisely to the little oasis wherein the children had taken refuge. Arrived at the entrance, they seemed to consult together for an instant; then resumed their way through the thorny tufts, rounded the mass of rock behind which the sisters had crouched, and stopped, with the words, "Here it is."

Francine, in dire alarm, had hidden her head upon Josèphe's knees; she, less timid, gently put aside the branches, and could then see a grave already dug in a gravelly portion of the soil. The infirmary-men had laid down the corpse upon the ground, wrapped-up in a coarse linen cloth. Then they took a sack, hidden under a projecting bit of rock, and emptied its contents into the grave. The white dust, that rose up from it as a cloud, was wafted to the children in a sour odour of lime. This was carefully spread over the bottom of the hole, so as to form a bed for the dead body, and was then sprinkled with water drawn from the sea. These preparatory measures had all been taken in gloomy silence. Nought was heard but the scraping of the spade upon the rocky soil, and the monotonous bubbling of the tiny waves that rippled with the evening breeze upon the shore. Josèphe, her neck out-stretched, her large eyes dilated, and with a painful sense of tightening at her heart-strings, continued on the watch.

At this moment, two of the bearers took up the body, and brought it close to the hole dug for its reception. They were separated from the children only by a tuft of bushes. As they lightly grazed it with their burden, a gust of wind unrolled one of the corners of the covering cloth; a livid head was visible by the last glimmering of light; and Josèphe uttered a stifled cry. The fall of the body into the pit prevented her being heard; but the moment's glance had sufficed—the child thought she recognized the face of Monsieur Gabriel. She threw herself back, in inexpressible horror. It was the first time that death had come before her eyes, and it appeared to her in a guise that filled her with grief and terror. Clinging to Francine, she began to tremble in every limb. The noise of the earth and flint-stones, that were shovelled into the grave, held her as one petrified. It was only when the four grave-diggers had left the ravine and disappeared in the pathway, that her agony found vent. Francine raised her head and asked what had happened; but receiving no reply, threw herself into Josèphe's arms, and began in turn to sob.

The distress of her little sister seemed to counteract that of Josèphe, who forced herself to stifle her own anguish, and began embracing and consoling

Francine.

—"Don't cry" stammered she, choking in spite of herself; "you mustn't be afraid, … you mustn't cry…."

—"What is the matter with you, Josey; what is it?" inquired the little one again, holding her sister's head between her own two hands, and kissing her moistened cheeks.

—"It's … nothing, … "returned Josèphe, her accent belying her words, … "I was taken by surprise…."

—"Have the men gone?" asked Francine, looking with frightened glance towards the grave.

—"You see they have," answered Josèphe shuddering.

—"What did they come here to do? They were carrying something. It was a dead body, wasn't it?"

Her sister put her hand upon her lips.

—"Don't talk of that, Zine!" murmured she, her sobs again overpowering her.

—"You saw it?" asked the child, frightened, yet curious.

—"Yes, O God!" faltered forth her sister in reply;
"… and … I knew it again … it was Monsieur
Gabriel!"

—"Your good friend, Josey?" cried Francine; "are you sure? And he's there … there, under the ground? … Oh! let's go, let's go; I'm afraid … I'm afraid!"

And again she threw herself into her sister's arms, who exerted herself to the utmost to re-assure her, and at the same time to control her own tears.

—"There, stop, Zine!" said she, with broken voice; "… we must be calm … we must dry up our eyes … or mother will be uneasy." Then raising herself suddenly, "Hark," she added, "I fancied I heard some one calling us; quick, quick, let's go up!"

With these words the two little maidens rose from the ground; quitting the ravine, they hastily regained the platform, trembling and out of breath when they reached it.

Geneviève was waiting there for them; but it was already dark, and this prevented her noticing their trouble. She took them by the hand, to lead them in, and made them repeat their joint prayers; both went to bed, without speaking of the adventure at the ravine.

III

Josèphe slept badly; and the next morning, when she got up, was pale and drooping. Geneviève, who did not fail to notice it, questioned her with nervous solicitude; but the child answered that nothing was the matter. Only, at every inquiry, her eyes filled with tears, and her voice trembled. Thus languidly for her did the day wear away. In the evening she was still more depressed, but still not suffering pain. She passed a restless night; and on the following morning Ropars went for the Surgeon of the lazaretto. He examined the child, and put several questions that darkened the brow of Mathieu. Geneviève, whose looks went direct from the Surgeon to her husband, perceived this; and she felt a blow stricken upon her heart. At the moment when the two crossed the thresh-hold, she followed, shut the door abruptly, and stopped them.

—"It is the … disease, … is it not?" she asked in anguish. She had not dared to name the yellow fever; the Surgeon seemed to hesitate in his reply.

—"Ah! I'm certain of it," she exclaimed, confirmed by this very hesitation; "so, our precautions have all been useless! The blow has come, and all is over!"

She could not avoid sinking down upon the stone bench, placed beside the door; and she covered her face with her apron. The Surgeon taxed himself to console her with vague assurances; but it was evident that he himself had no longer confidence in his efforts. Overcome by the implacable power of the contagion, he persevered in struggling against it, without hope and from a sense of duty, as soldiers, for the honour of their flag, defend silently a post that has been abandoned. So, perceiving that his words, far from soothing the grief of Geneviève, did but redouble it, he turned towards the keeper, and, having briefly repeated to him some directions already given for the child, he went his way.

Ropars remained some moments on one spot, with his arms crossed and his head upon his breast; but a still deeper groan from Geneviève caused him to raise his eyes. He took her hand.

—"It isn't time for despair yet," said he, with gentle firmness; "when God shall have decided against us, your whole life-time will be left for grief. At present, let us devote ourselves to our duty, and follow strictly the injunctions of the doctor."

—"And he has told us nothing at all!" said the mother, who at heart felt half-incensed against the Surgeon, for not having more vigorously combatted her fears; "he has not given us any hope!"

—"God is the master," replied Mathieu, in all simplicity, "and so long as he has not declared his pleasure, we may believe that all will work well; but if the darling creature must be taken from our hands, let us at least to the last moment show him, how keen is our desire to keep her."

Hereupon the feverish voice of the child reached their ears.

—"Hark, she's calling me!" cried Geneviève, rising in urgent haste to go in. Ropars stopped her.

—"Dry your eyes first," said he, passing his own hand with fond compassion over the poor mother's moistened eyelids; "Josèphe mustn't think that you are anxious. Don't you know that her life may depend on this?"

—"Yes, yes," she answered, "fear not, Mathieu, I will not cry any more;" and she forcibly restrained the tears that were filling her eyes afresh… "Look, no one would notice it now… And the doctors, besides, may be mistaken, mayn't they?… And after all, God will have pity on us."

—"We must hope so," replied the keeper, much moved; "but if it is his part to have pity, it is ours to show resignation. Bear up, then, good heart; go to the child with a smile; it will do her good; and first of all … kiss me … that we may keep up each other's resolution."

Josèphe's mother threw her arms around her husband's neck, and gave way to a new flood of tears. But she checked them at the sound of the sick one's voice calling her for the second time, and, by a supreme effort thrusting down her despair into the very depths of her heart, she rushed into the house with calm brow and a smile upon her lips.

Josèphe, nevertheless, grew rapidly worse. In the evening the fever was doubly hot upon her. One after another, she spoke of sister Francine, of Michael, of the cherry-tree in blossom, and of her good friend Monsieur Gabriel. At one moment she fancied that she heard the last-named; she called him; she wished to know if he had brought her the promised presents. At another time, the scene in the ravine appeared to be vividly in her recollection; she cried out that Monsieur Gabriel was dead; and she heard the earth grating over him in the pit. The Surgeon came to see her repeatedly, and multiplied his prescriptions, without power to arrest the onward march of the disease. That night was an awful one for the hapless mother; she kept her child clasped in her arms, the little one's mind wandering more and more. At sunrise the turbulent delirium was over, to give place to the torpor that precedes death. At length, towards the middle of the day, Josèphe opened her eyes, and uttered one sigh—it was the last.

The blow had been so decidedly expected, that the despair of Ropars and of

Geneviève could scarcely be violent. The bitterness of their loss had, so to say, preceded it; both had tasted it, drop by drop, during the protracted agony. And yet the mother's calmness had in it a something haggard, that would have startled a looker-on less troubled than Mathieu himself. Bent upon rendering the last offices to her daughter, she was long occupied in combing out her beautiful black hair; she dressed the body in her best clothes, and laid it out with the hands crossed over the breast, as Josèphe had been used to carry them when asleep. All this was done slowly, tranquilly, with a sort of complacency even, and often intermingled with kisses. It was but at intervals that a tear trickled over her cheeks, that were marbled with glowing spots; it was but a slight trembling that shook the hand, as it performed its sorrowful duty. At length, when she who had brought this child into the world, and who had nourished it with her milk and with her affection, had herself sewed it up in its shroud, she went to the window, broke the stalk of a gilly-flower—the only one that the sea-winds had spared—pulled off its leaves, and scattered them over the winding sheet.

In the meantime, night had fallen. Deposited at the head of the darkened alcove, the dead form might indistinctly be traced through its covering of linen, as though it were sketched in marble. Higher up hung a Christ, in ivory, the head bent forward, and the arms extended. Geneviève knelt down near the bed, and remained there for a long time, with her head leaning upon her joined hands. Half-aloud she murmured a prayer; but whilst her lips repeated faithfully every word, their meaning was not taken in by her mind. When she had finished it, she raised herself up mechanically, and looked about her; her brain was a gloomy chaos. Putting up both hands to her forehead, she pressed it, with a stifled cry, as though she sought to stay that whirlwind of confused and lacerating thoughts. There was, for some few moments, a struggle between her will and her despair; finally the former gained the ascendant; she stepped towards the door and opened it.

Her husband had taken refuge on the platform with Francine, to remove her from the harrowing sight of placing the body in its shroud. Geneviève could see him standing near the parapet; the little girl was at his feet, with her head resting on his knees. Since the death of her sister, she had not spoken a word. Fixed in one place, with eyes dilated and lips compressed, she seemed to be endeavouring to comprehend what had occurred. Her two small hands hung down inactive, and her naked feet appeared to be glued to the ground. Seeing her thus, under the early rays of the moon that were playing in her light-coloured tresses, Geneviève was, as it were, brought back to herself. A flash passed across the blankness of her expression; her nostrils dilated; a flood of tears gushed from her eyes. Springing towards the child, she seized it in her arms with a sort of doleful passionateness, to which Francine at once and amply responded, by an outburst of sobs and caresses. For a long time there was nothing but an interchange of broken appeals and unfinished phrases. The little girl would go on asking for her sister, while the mother, whose despair was revived by such demands, compelled herself to smother them beneath her kisses. At last, her strength exhausted, she let her arms, that upheld Francine, drop down, and felt that she was gently withdrawn from her. It was Mathieu, who placed the child upon the ground. He then led the mother a little further apart, and obliged her to sit down upon the stone-bench, leaning her back against the parapet. She tried to raise herself up, as she stretched out her hands.

—"My child!" she stammered through her sobbings; "I want my child!"

—"In good time thou shalt see her," said Ropars, who according to the custom of the Bretagne peasantry only *thee'd* and *thou'd* Geneviève, when under the influence of strong emotion; "but first thou must listen with all attention, for what I have to tell thee is of the deepest consequence."

—"Ah! I would, I would!" was her reply, putting both hands up to her head; "but don't be hurt, Mathieu, if it be impossible. I hear yonder, look you, something that hushes up all the rest; it is her death-rattle, my good man!... And ... do you know?... I like the anguish that it causes me, to hear it; I can fancy that there still is breath in her. Oh! Jesus! who would have told me, that I should yearn after the dying breath of my child?" Ropars laid a hand upon the head of the miserable woman, whose sobbings had recommenced.

—"Be soothed at heart," he said to her with touching firmness; "the good God wills that we should submit, and not thus give way. The dead one is now in her Paradise, where she has no more need of us; but she leaves behind her a sister, whose life is in our charge."

—"How do you mean?" asked Geneviève, raising towards him her eyes, in which alarm had arrested the tears.

—"Don't you understand?" returned the keeper, lowering his voice; "the breath of the disease is like the sea-wind; it spares no one; and it may send, at any instant, the living to rejoin the dead."

—"Heavenly Saviour! is this a warning?" demanded Geneviève, clasping her hands. "Must this child too, be struck down?... Have you remarked any thing?... Ah! tell the truth, Mathieu, tell it at once; I would rather be killed at one blow."

—"So far, the child suffers from nothing but her distress," rejoined Ropars; "but if she remains in this deadly air, who can guarantee us that she will escape?"

—"Evil upon us!" cried Geneviève, raising her joined hands over her head; "why did you remind me of it, Mathieu? I did not wish to think of it; and now I shall see her dying, every hour. God forgive you for thus turning the blade that is within my heart!"

—"If I touch it, it is but to withdraw it," was the quarter-master's answer. "It won't do now to shut one's eyes and let the squall overtake us; we must work ship with all our might for the little one's safety.... If she remains on the island, you have too many chances of sewing up her winding-sheet, Geneviève; she must leave it forthwith."

—"But how?"

Ropars threw his eyes around him, to satisfy himself that he was not overheard.

—"There is a way," he replied cautiously.

—"The powder-magazine skiff?"

—"No!"

—"The gun-boat?"

—"She's there, you know, to keep guard over the island."

—"But who then can help us?"

—"The tide."

Geneviève looked at her husband, but without understanding what he meant.

—"It is now high-water," continued Mathieu; "in less than an hour the sea will have gone down enough to leave only four feet of water upon the line of reefs that runs from Trébéron to the Ile des Morts. With courage, and by the help of God, the passage may be tried. I am going to carry the child over to Dorot."

And as the mother could not restrain a cry of terror;—"Speak lower, unhappy one!" he added vehemently; "are you desirous of betraying me? Except the Superintendent of the powder-magazine and myself, no one knows the way. We have often passed along it when we were fishing together, and always passed it safely."

—"But not at night," interrupted Geneviève; "not burdened with a child."

—"The child weighs scarcely anything, and the moon is full," replied Ropars somewhat impatiently. "Besides, I have been thinking of it all the evening; and there is no other means. My mind is made up, and I shall do what must be done, happen what may. Your remarks may lessen my confidence, but cannot hold me back. Try rather, then, to brace up my nerves, as is the duty of a brave wife, and to prepare the child to go. When the outer point of the high rock is bare, it will be time for me to make the attempt, and for you to pray God that he may open us a way of safety in the sea."

The quarter-master's tone was so determined, that Geneviève saw at once the uselessness of resistance. With little will of his own in the ordinary transactions of life, Mathieu rarely formed a resolution; but, once decided on, he maintained it immovably. Moreover, when the first shock was passed, his explanations and assurances somewhat tranquillized Francine's mother, and indeed half convinced her. There remained the child, whose opposition or fright was apprehended by Ropars. Geneviève went and raised her up from the ground, and the father and the mother seated her upon their knees, which they purposely placed close together.

—"You want to see the cherry-tree in blossom, don't you?" said the former, embracing her.

—"Not any more, now," was the low-toned reply.

—"Nay, nay, it is just the time," added the poor mother with an effort; "over there, you will be more at liberty ... happier ... you'll have Michael for a play-fellow."

—"No," said the child with changing voice, "I would rather stay with Josèphe."

Geneviève clasped her hands and closed her eyes; speech failed her. It was Ropars' turn. Drawing Francine close up to his breast, and whispering in her ear,

—"Listen," said he; "we are in trouble. You would not wish to make it worse, would you? You love us too well for that."

In place of answer, the child threw both her arms about her father's neck, and pressed her little rosy cheek against the wrinkled cheek of the mariner.

—"Yes, yes, I was certain of it," continued Mathieu; "and you will do whatever we ask you?"

Francine made an affirmative sign.

—"Well, then," Ropars went on, "you must go and pass a few days with Uncle Dorot; and as we have no boat, I am going to carry you over the passage. Won't you be quiet in the middle of the sea, when you have papa's shoulders for a skiff?"

The child shuddered.—"I would rather stay," said she, in hurried accents.

—"But that's impossible," rejoined the father; "I want to carry you to the powder-magazine. It must be so, and we are to set out directly. But if you are not brave, if you think of calling out, the way will be harder, and perhaps something serious may happen to me. Do you understand?"

—"Yes ... yes ... I won't go," replied the little girl, beginning to tremble.

Geneviève drew her once more into her arms. "Hush, hush!" said she, laying her lips upon Francine's hair, and rocking her upon her breast, "children ought to obey.... God has ordained it ... do what you are bidden ... for your papa, ... for me ... for Josèphe.... If she could speak she would tell you to be good and obedient.... Would you make her sorrowful in Heaven?"

—"Oh! no," cried the child, throwing herself again into Mathieu's arms.

—"Then you will come?" asked he.

—"Yes," murmured the little girl.

—"And you won't be afraid; you won't say a word?"

—"No."

—"Let's be going then!" exclaimed the keeper, who had got up and was looking over the parapet. "The high rock is out of water; we mustn't wait any longer."

He took Francine in his arms and went rapidly down one of the foot-paths leading to the shore of the islet. Geneviève followed, in inexpressible anguish. All three reached a rocky point that stretched far out into the waters. It was the extremity of the line of reefs that connected the powder-magazine with Tréberon. Ropars placed the child on the ground, in order to take note of his direction. The passage, under the rays of the moon, was tinged with pale green, varied by small lines of white that were made by the light fringe of foam upon the waves. So gentle were their undulations, that one might have fancied a field of green wheat chequered with white camomile flowers. Beyond, the Ile des Morts in all its breadth was illumined by the moonlight, with its yellowish buildings, its long slated roofs, and its lightning-rods, standing out against the sky. So calm was the night that the sentry's step was heard, as he paced up and down before the watch-box of granite, built at the corner of the esplanade. At the forked head of the two islands, and partially in shadow, lay the silent gun-boat, balancing at anchor.

Ropars examined every thing with scrupulous attention. He pointed out to Geneviève the direction of the submarine causeway, indicated by a faint shadow on the surface of the water, as he threw aside his waistcoat and hat; then taking both of his wife's hands, who looked at him with haggard eyes,
—"the time is come, Geneviève," said he; "kiss me, and pray the good God to be with us."

The poor woman responded at first to his embrace, without power to utter a word; but when she felt that he had disengaged himself and was returning towards the child, a cry escaped her; she was not mistress of herself. She forgot all that Mathieu had said to her, all that she herself had promised, and encircled him with her arms in all the desperation of terror.

—"You shall not go," she stammered out, "you shall not go!... It is rushing on to death ... in the name of your marriage-vow, remain to be my succour, my companion!... Would you then leave me here alone with Josèphe?... Look, how broad the sea is, and how deep! You and Francine, you will be lost in it!... Ah! if it be God's will, let us all die here; but at least let us die together! Mathieu, I will not have you quit me; you shall not carry off my child; you shall not go!"

Ropars endeavoured to calm her, and struggled to release himself from her hold; but she clung to him, and refused to hear a word. And as he recalled to her that she had, a minute before, induced Francine's consent,

—"I was wrong," she wildly interrupted him; "I will no longer have it so. If you leave me, I will follow; and you will be responsible before God for what may happen. Mathieu, do not tempt me! Mathieu, have pity on me!… What have I done to you, that you should thus go voluntarily to destruction? Do you no longer care for life with me?… Ah! if I have failed in my duty, be not angry with me, dear soul! If my too great anguish has offended you, forgive me! I will not cry any more; I will be every thing that you desire. Hold; look on me rather; forgive me; but say that you will stay."

She had sunk down upon her knees, and held Ropars' hands pressed firmly against her lips. He exerted himself to raise her up.

—"Enough, Geneviève," said he, in a tone wherein commiseration disputed with impatience; "I thought that you were braver…. This is not what you promised me. Think, think, unhappy woman, that the time is passing away!"

Geneviève groaned, and recommenced the same entreaties. He cast an anxious look towards the sea, and saw that the farthest jags of the high rock were dry. Longer delay would increase the danger, and might render the passage impossible. Mathieu seized Geneviève sharply by the elbows, and raised her upon her feet, with her face opposite his own.

—"On your salvation, listen!" said he, in accent so decided that she trembled at it; "this is the first time that I have reminded you that I am your master, and, if you be not wiser, it will perhaps be the last; but by the God who saved us, you shall obey, and that without further discussion! The child's life is to be preserved; nothing can stay me now. Remain there, I solemnly command you, and make not one step, nor utter one single cry, or, so surely as I am my mother's son, I will never forgive you, even until the day of Judgment!"

At these words, he seated Geneviève, petrified by the shock, ran to his little daughter, whom he took upon his shoulders, and dashed with her into the waves.

When Geneviève turned round, at the noise made by his plunge into the water, Ropars was on the causeway of the submerged reefs, and the waves were rolling against his breast. She tried to get up; but her strength failed her, and she could but utter a feeble cry. Mathieu heard it and looked back. He could see through the moonlight the indistinct form of Geneviève who, half- lying down upon the rock, was wringing her joined hands as though towards him. He found his heart, which he had steeled by an effort of will, sinking within him in pity for her. Taking note of the waters, green and deep, whose abysses were opening around him, hearing over his head the breathings of the child who panted with terror, and thinking that the hapless creature from whom they had just parted violently might perchance never see them more, there came across him a feeling of commiseration so tender, that tears almost filled his eyes; he paused, in spite of himself, in the midst of the murmuring waves, turned his head backwards towards the shore, and called to her in a voice, restrained but full of gentleness—"Don't cry Geneviève; and God bless you! all will go well."

Then, without waiting for an answer, which he feared might unman him, he went on his way, his eyes fixed upon the line along the water that marked the direction of the reef. Soon, however, he ceased to distinguish that particular appearance of the waves which rendered it easy to trace this line from the shore. Immersed in the sea, he no longer saw anything beyond him, but a surface uniform and agitated, without any distinctive movement or colour. He was therefore compelled to shape his course direct for the rock on the Ile des Morts whereon the causeway abutted, and which with its pointed ridges was visible, far-away in the obscurity.

Armed with a broken boat-hook, Mathieu sounded at each step that he took; but notwithstanding all his care, the difficulty of his course increased at every moment. The unevenness of the rocks exposed him to incessant stumbling. Lifted off his feet by the waves, half-stunned by the deep rumbling noise that was around him, groping along a path irregular and strange to him and bounded on either side by an abyss, he advanced with the greatest deliberation, his strong will controlling his impatience, and his whole soul rivetted upon his every movement. His fixed gaze sought to pierce the liquid veil of the waters; his hands glued to the boat-hook seemed to long to solder it to the reef; his feet, in an agony of search, seemed to force themselves to guess at their path, before they would select it. Thus he reached the middle of the passage, where he came into the neighbourhood of the gun-boat. All there was silent; nothing stirred. The cries of "Watch, Watch!" uttered at intervals by the look-out at each cat-head, had for some time ceased to be heard; their two shadows even were not perceptible, for they had long been immovable at their post. Certain that their look-out was altogether needless, the sailors on watch were without doubt asleep.

Mathieu, who was afraid that they might awake, was anxious to avoid this danger by hurrying on; but at the very moment when he came within the shadow thrown, abaft the gun-boat, over the glittering waters, his footing of rock failed him by suddenly shelving downwards. Francine felt him sinking, as a vessel that founders, and the waves washed up over her hair. She could not restrain a piercing shriek.

Her father, in extreme alarm, lowered her down against his breast, and pressed one hand upon her lips. But it was too late; the cry had undoubtedly been overheard, for a shadow immediately rose up, forward, and the noise of footsteps echoed along the deck. Ropars had but time to throw himself under the taffrail of the stationary vessel, and to grasp a boom, whereto he remained suspended.

One of the sailors on watch came aft, and was immediately joined by his comrade.

—"The devil take me, if I didn't hear a cry," said the former.

—"Pardieu! it half-woke me up," added the second.

—"But I've looked about, and it's no use; I don't see any thing."

—"Nor I."

The couple were leaning over the sea, which kept up its gentle murmurings, and on which only light undulations were visible, fringed with half-phosphorescent foam. The second man of the watch seemed all at once to be seized with inquietude, that caused his voice to tremble.

—"I say, Morvan," he cautiously began, "those Roscanvel and Lanvoc barks haven't passed by, without leaving some christian soul under water here—don't you think so?"

—"Why so?" asked Morvan.

—"Why so?" returned the sailor, who seemed half-afraid and half-ashamed; "why, parbleu! ... you know what they say ... I didn't invent it ... there are some people who tell you that shipwrecked men, dying in mortal sin, leave their souls upon the waves that drowned them: and that every year, on the day and at the exact time of the accident, they utter a cry of anguish, just by way of asking prayers for themselves."

—"And you believe that, you, Lascar?" said Morvan with a laugh more blustering than assured.

—"It isn't I," rejoined the sailor, "it's our mess-mates.... But, none the less, the voice wasn't like any body else's; it was sharp and thin, as one might say that of a child."

—"Get out, nonsense!" interrupted the first seaman, evidently disquieted by his comrade's explanation; "you see there's nothing more to be heard, and there is nothing afloat but the moonlight, and the night-chill that will make us sneeze. It's well that we both kept our allowance of wine. Come on, let's go and drink it; that'll put your morality into trim again."

The two sailors went off. After waiting a moment, Mathieu replaced the child on his shoulders, enjoined strict silence, at the same time cheering her up, and let go the boom for the purpose of regaining the causeway; but he had lost the direction, and his feet encountered only empty space. Forced to swim with his precious burden, he hoped that a few fathoms' distance would bring him back to his pathway on the reefs; he had already gone beyond it. Fresh attempts were not more successful; and twenty times did he renew his search, finding only, at each, deep water.

Frightened and panting for breath, he swam about without aim, endeavouring to touch ground, and no longer able to distinguish the Ile des Morts from Trébéron. After having long shifted his course, struggled against the tide in which every moment he plunged still deeper, been a thousand times brought back from despair to hope, and run the full length of his endurance and his courage, he felt at last that he was overcome. His respiration grew painful, his eyes were covered with a film; all things were to him but as a revolving chaos; his mind wandered. A moment more, and he and Francine had disappeared beneath the waters. The gun-boat, which he had wished to avoid, but which he could no longer perceive, was his sole means of safety. He summoned all his remaining strength to utter a cry for help; a surge, more powerful, stifled it on his lips. Half-fainting and having nothing left him but that instinctive self-defence which survives the will, he struggled still an instant, buffeted from wave to wave; then felt that he was going down. But all at once, he was arrested; his feet had fallen on to the reef; they were fastened on it, and steadied themselves thereon; his body straightened up; the water that blinded him seemed to lower itself. He took breath and looked before him, and could see at the distance of a hundred steps the cleft rock of the Ile des Morts. A few minutes sufficed for reaching it. Touching the shore he fell down upon it, and called Francine with expiring voice. The child, terrified, could only reply by throwing herself upon his breast, where he held her for some time in his embrace. His first thought had been for her; his second carried him back to Geneviève who was expecting his return, to know that they were safe. Still tottering, he raised himself up, took his little daughter by the hand, and set himself to climbing the steep slope that led to the terrace.

It was necessary to make the tour of the powder magazine, to avoid the sentinel placed at the angle which commanded the main roadside; and also, on reaching the magazine keeper's door, to knock gently, for fear of being heard from without. Dorot fortunately had the light sleep of old soldiers; he awoke at the first knocking, and appeared at the window.

—"Open the door!" said Mathieu to him in a low voice.

—"Ropars!" cried the sergeant, thunderstruck.

—"Lower! and be quick!" returned the seaman "our lives' safety is at stake."

Dorot went down rapidly, drew back the bolt, and made them enter the house. Mathieu paused, when across the thresh-hold, with the child pressed against his knees.

—"Heaven protect us! whence come you, Ropars?" inquired the sergeant.

—"You see," replied the sailor, "we have come out of the sea, and we have crossed over it, to come hither."

Dorot drew back, exclaiming, "Can it be? in God's name, what has happened, that you should thus expose your life?"

—"It has happened," rejoined Mathieu, "that Josèphe died this morning of the contagion! ... that"—

—"What's that you say?"

—"'Tis just so, Dorot; and as Geneviève and I were anxious to save the other one, I have brought her to you."

—"And Heaven reward you for the thought!" said the sergeant; "the child is dearly welcome."

He had offered his hand to Mathieu; but the latter did not take it.

—"Think well what it is I am asking you," said he; "perhaps the child may be bringing here disease and desolation upon you!"

"I hope there will be nothing of the kind," returned Dorot; "but God's will be done!"

—"Bear in mind also," continued the quarter-master, insisting, "that if the thing gets wind, you run a risk of punishment for having violated the quarantine."

—"Then the will of man be done!" was the sergeant's simple observation.

—"But still think."

—"Of nothing further, Ropars," interrupted the sergeant; "there! enough said —too much. No words about the matter; you have brought me the little one; I accept her."

He had stooped down to Francine, whom he then took up in his arms, and with her remounted to the small chamber formerly occupied by Geneviève. He, himself, stripped off from the child her dripping clothes, and put her to sleep in an old cot of Michael's.

The father, who had followed them, remained at the door with his arms hanging down at his side, the very picture of gratitude deeply felt, but unable to vent itself in words. Only, when Dorot turned round towards him, he seized one of his hands and held it silently grasped. Dorot, who desired to avoid a scene, began at once to talk of the means of concealing the little girl's change of abode. It was sufficient that her absence from Trébéron would not be remarked; as for her being at the Ile des Morts, it could not give rise to any suspicion, since the guard of artillery that did duty at the magazine, and that might have been surprised at this increase in the keeper's family, was to be changed on the following day. Ropars arranged certain signals for transmitting mutually the news between the neighbour islands. These were to be renewed several times a day, and thus relieve them at least from the anguish of uncertainty. At length, when all had been agreed upon, Mathieu drew near the window and looked out. The breeze had freshened, the sky appeared less starry, and a transparent vapour was beginning to creep over the sea.

—"It is time to start," said he, returning towards the sergeant; "may God pay you for what you do, Dorot! As for Geneviève and myself, we shall remain your debtors to all eternity."

—"We'll talk of that, by and by," replied the keeper; "just now, the main thing, and that which troubles me, is the passage over."

—"Don't be uneasy about that," answered Ropars; "now that the child is in safety, I shall cross the channel just as easily as one goes to church. The limbs are firm when the heart doesn't tremble. But I wish I were already on the other side; I've stayed here too long for Geneviève, who is looking for me."

—"Away, then! if it must be," cried the sergeant; "but for God's sake, Ropars, be careful, and don't forget that you have two lives to save with your own."

—"I'll do all that a man can do," returned the quarter-master; "and believe me, cousin, I've no desire to die this night!... But too much talk; the time is slipping away; I mustn't wait for the change of tide."

He went up to Francine's cot, to take leave of her; but the child, wearied out by so many emotions, had dropped off to sleep. One of her arms was doubled beneath her head, and lost in the loosened tresses of her golden hair; the other, folded on her breast, pressed to it a little relic formerly given to Geneviève who, in her superstitious motherly devotedness, had deprived herself of it that it might be a safe-guard for her child. Although her breathing was equal and easy, still was it broken at intervals by a long drawn sigh; whilst her cheeks, that in her sleep were beginning to re-assume their rosy tint, still showed some traces of tears. Mathieu looked at her for some moments in touching silence; then bending himself slowly down, imprinted a light kiss upon

Francine's tiny hand, then one upon her hair, then one upon her cheek. Without opening her eyes, the child made a gesture of annoyance; he stood up.

—"Yes, yes, there, sleep, poor creature of a merciful God!" he half-muttered; "I will not wake you."

Once more he seemed to enwrap her in a look overflowing with tenderness; then returned to Dorot, and took his hand.

—"I bequeath her to you, cousin," said he, moved in the extreme; "no one knows what may happen. Only … I can trust in your kindly heart, and if ever the child should become an orphan…."

—"Now God preserve her from it!" the sergeant took him up; "but if such misfortune should occur to her, Mathieu, you know well that she would become Michael's sister."

—"Thanks!" abruptly broke in the seaman; "that's exactly what I was longing to hear…. And now I set out calmly. I am prepared for every thing."

—"But you shan't set out thus, shivering and pulled down," objected the sergeant; "you must take something to cheer up your spirits."

—"Nothing," said Ropars, eagerly; "you have given me all that can give me strength, in giving me the assurance that the child will not remain unaided. Providence will do the rest. Your hand! and good-bye till we meet—here, or elsewhere!"

They heartily embraced; then Mathieu went down to the shore, and committed himself again to the waters. Although the tide had begun to rise, the passage was effected without overmuch danger. He reached, unharmed, the high rock of Trébéron which the floodtide had already encroached upon, and he ran to the place where he had left Geneviève. She was there no longer.

Astonished that she should not have awaited his return, he rapidly mounted the foot-path, reached his door, and called aloud. There was no reply. The darkness did not allow him to distinguish any thing. He groped his way to the hearth, and threw around him the trembling light of a lamp hurriedly lighted. Attracted to the alcove, his glance soon made out, beside the white form of the dead sewed up in its shroud, the outline of another and a larger form, extended without moving. Mathieu approached in agony. It was Geneviève in a swoon.

IV.

Thanks to the Surgeon's skill, Ropars' wife at length regained her senses; but it was to fall into convulsive spasms, followed by the annihilation of all her faculties. The whole day passed without her shaking off the torpor that belonged at once to sleep and to death. One might have said that so many shocks had snapped asunder her existence, and that the quiverings of life, still flitting across her state of languor, were but the movements of a machine on the point of stopping. However, towards evening, the fever declared itself. The patient passed insensibly from lethargy to delirious agitation; she did but recognize Mathieu at intervals; and falling back, with her senses, upon her sorrows, she soon fell again into wandering.

None of these symptoms seemed to belong to the malady that ravaged the lazaretto; and the Surgeon, disconcerted, let Mathieu divine his inability to make it out. Accustomed to the coarse medicines required by the robust patients of our ships, he was perforce a stranger, as are all like him, to the ailments of more delicate natures. Thus did he stand baffled before this woman, dying of a disorder such as he vainly sought to trace in his experiences. He could not conceal his doubts, and his need of more enlightened advice. Science, to which these mysterious and redoubtable symptoms were familiarized, might find there an index, where he perceived only confusion, and point out a remedy, which he dared but essay at hap- hazard.

This avowal, wrung from his loyal truth, was for Mathieu a new source of torture. Shut up within prescribed limits which forbid strangers to approach Trébéron, he could not invoke that experience to which Geneviève might perchance owe her safety. In vain did he see, at his feet, boats for transporting him across the sea, and on the horizon a town whence aid might be brought to him; an obstacle invincible and insurmountable linked him to his source of trouble.

Two whole days passed away for him, as one long agony, in alternations of mute dejection and of furious despair. After sitting for several hours at the bedside of the dying woman, when he saw the fever that had been lulled for an instant now returning with increased force, he ran down to the edge of the reefs, gazed upon the waters in the midst of which he found himself imprisoned, upon the armed vessel that guarded the passage, upon the ravines of the island dotted with graves recently dug, and pressing his closed fists against his forehead he cursed the day on which he had accepted this voluntary imprisonment. Angrily did he call God to account for the blows with which he was stricken; then, restored to his religious faith, he joined his hands, and with tears besought the Almighty to spare Geneviève.

Towards the morning of the third day, he had cause for believing that his prayers had been heard. The fever abated, and the patient recovered all her clearness of mind. But this change did not induce her to share the delight or the hopes of Mathieu.

—"Never believe that this is a cure, dear soul," said she in tones scarcely audible, and alternating every phrase with periods of silence; "the disease is going ... but it carries all with it.... That evening, when you went across the channel ... when I heard the child's cry from out of the sea itself ... I thought it was all over with you both ... and then ... I can't say what took place ... but it seemed to me ... that within me ... the main string of life was snapped.... So I feel now, that it's all over."

Ropars combatted these fears, repeating that the Surgeon was encouraged, and that all would go well. Geneviève, whose eyes were closed, raised the lids with difficulty and threw a glance upon him that was full of melancholy sweetness.

—"God is the master, Mathieu," said she; "he knows whether I am happy in living with you.... Only, ... believe me, poor husband, and don't rejoice too much ... it were wiser to expect the worst."

—"It were wiser," interrupted the quarter-master, "to take rest, and have confidence. I, too, trust in what I feel. This very night, I had a weight of lead upon my heart; it is light now; I can breathe in one single breath. In God's name, let your health be restored to you, and be anxious for a continuance of life, if it were but for my sake."

Geneviève made an effort to lay her cold and moistened hand upon that of Ropars.

—"You are good, Mathieu," said she, letting fall two little tears, the last that emotion could drain from eyes already exhausted with weeping. "Ah me! my chief regret now is at not having always thought of this ... at not having shown myself sufficiently grateful.... Heavens! how much worthier we should be of those we love, if we did but remember that some day we must leave them.... Since my mind has returned, this idea has haunted me; I now perceive all my faults; ... I feel remorse for them.... Oh! tell me in mercy, Mathieu, do you forgive me now ... for never having been what I ought to have been?"

—"Talk not so, Geneviève," said the seaman quickly, and with deep feeling; "you know well that I could not have asked from God a better wife. Since you have been mine, I have wanted for nothing; it is I who should be grateful to you."

—"No, no," replied the sick woman with increasing animation; "many a time have I lacked courage and patience.... Not with you alone ... but with

Francine … with Josèphe! … poor child of my heart, who had so few years to live!… And to think, Mathieu, that I have often made her cry! … her, who is now beneath the ground!… Ah! it is the tears of the dead that weigh heavily here…. And other persons, whom I may have injured … and God against whom I have sinned!… Cannot I then hope for mercy?"

Then, as if this idea had awakened in her a sort of terror:

—"Ah! it is impossible!" added she, sitting up; "Mathieu, Mathieu, I must see a confessor!"

—"But how to get him here?" said the quarter-master sorrowfully; "have you forgotten that the island is in quarantine?"

—"What! not to be able to save even one's soul?" returned Geneviève, clasping her hands. "Alas! am I then doomed to die without reconciliation? My God! what is to be done? The most miserable sinner is allowed to confess his sins, and to ask absolution for them; my God! must I alone remain without help?"

She stopped abruptly, putting up both hands to her forehead.

—"Ah! I remember now," she resumed; "have you not told me that on board your ships, when at the moment of death no priest was to be had, any Christian might take his place? … that God looked to the intention?"

—"I have said so," replied Ropars, "and all the seamen hereabouts will tell you the same thing, upon the assurance of their pastors."

—"Then," replied the dying woman, turning towards the seaman her eye lustrous with the fever, "I desire to confess myself to you!"

She raised herself upon her elbow, and crossed herself. Mathieu seemed overwhelmed, but could make no objection to her will. As we have remarked, he belonged to that race almost extinct, even in Brittany, in whom still existed the earnest and the simple faith of other days. Often, on occasion of shipwreck, men such as he might have been seen, after exhausting all means of saving themselves, to kneel down in the expectation of death, and confess themselves one to another, as did the ancient cavaliers on the eve of combat. Therefore was he more troubled than surprised at the request of Geneviève; and when he heard her murmur the prayer that precedes confession, he took off his hat and made the sign of the cross, ready to fulfill the holy office that necessity had entrusted to him.

And something mournful and touching was it. The early dawn of day light doubtfully illumined the alcove; the dishevelled head of Geneviève was bent towards the grizzled head of Mathieu; and one might have heard the murmur of that supremest confidence carried on in lowered voice, often interrupted by the failure of the dying woman's strength, or by the seaman's entreaties that she would curtail it. But she persisted in resuming it, with the determination peculiar to those severe consciences which are never satisfied with their self-accusations. At length, when she had concluded, Ropars detached the ivory crucifix from the head of the bed; he approached it to the lips of Geneviève, and placing his hand upon her brow with mournful solemnity,

—"May God pardon thee as I do to the utmost of my power," said he; "and if it be not his will that thou shouldst live for my happiness, may he provide for thee a place in his Paradise!"

Her face assumed an expression of ineffable serenity.

—"Thanks," murmured she; "your absolution shall prevail before the Trinity, Mathieu; now I feel at peace."

A ray of sunlight creeping in through the window-curtain reached her bed; she turned round.

—"It is day," continued she; "I did not hope to see another.... God has given me a respite!... He is willing that I should taste of the latest joy that I looked for upon earth ... nor will you refuse it to me, Mathieu?"

—"Ask it, Geneviève," said the mariner; "what man can do, I will do."

She took his hand and looked at him.

—"You have told me, haven't you, that cousin could see and make out your signals?"

—"Yes, and it is true."

—"Then by all the affection you bear me, Mathieu, I beseech you to signalize him at once to bring Francine out upon his terrace; when she is there, you will take me in your arms, you will carry me to the high rock, and if God grant me grace, I shall reach it with still life enough left to see my child once more, and to embrace her in spirit."

—"It shall be done so as you desire, Geneviève," said the quarter-master, who, impressed by the presentiments of the dying one, had abandoned hope, and had not strength to refuse her anything.

—"Quickly, then, very quickly!... for I feel that God is calling me."

Ropars rushed out, as though he feared there would scarcely be time; but he came in again almost in a moment, exclaiming that Francine was already on the terrace of the magazine with Dorot. Stretching out her hands to him, the dying woman uttered a feeble cry of joy. He wrapped her up in his winter-cape, and carried her gently in his arms as far as the parapet of their platform.

—"Where is she?" inquired Geneviève, her eyes blinded by the light of day, and trying in vain to look steadily; "I can't make out anything, Mathieu! where is the child: show me the child!"

—"Look down there at our feet," replied the seaman; "can you see the high rock?"

—"Yes."

—"Can you follow the bubbling of the sea along the reef?"

—"Yes, yes."

—"And away, yonder, over the reefs, can you distinguish the stone-work of the terrace?"

—"Down there? … no … there's only a cloud! I can see nothing…. Oh! if it be too late!… if she be there under my very eyes, and I can no longer see her! … My God, my God, once more, only once, let me see my child!"

These words, or rather these mother's cries, had been so full of sadness, that Ropars could not restrain his tears. He seated his sinking wife upon the parapet, and himself kneeled down to support her.

—"Courage, Geneviève!" he stammered out; "look well to this side … between the line of the sea and the sky."

—"I am looking," said Geneviève, appearing in the effort to rally all the life left in her "…. Raise my head, Mathieu … screen me from the sun…."

She checked herself with a stifled exclamation.

—"Ah! there she is! there she is!… She sees me … she is lifting up her arms…. Francine … my daughter … my child!"

So impulsively did she lean forward, that but for Ropars, she would have thrown herself upon the rocks that sloped down to the sea. A flitting ray of life had lighted up her features; she sent kisses on her fingers to the child, and talked to it as though it could hear her; she raised her hands to Heaven, with rapid and broken ejaculations; she smiled and wept at once. Finally, her strength failed to endure so great emotion, and her head fell upon the quarter-master's shoulder. In alarm, he took her again in his arms, to carry her back into the house; but she made signs to him that she wished to remain out-doors. He laid her down upon the bench, whereon the family had been used to sit together in the evening, in front of the sea, which was now lighted up by the rising sun. After a swoon that lasted some time, she opened her eyes, and asked for her daughter. Mathieu looked towards the powder magazine and said that Dorot had taken her away. She bowed her head with sorrowing resignation.

—"He has done right," she went on, in feeble accents; ... "besides, I feel ... that my sight grows thick.... I couldn't see her any more ... and ... I still have something to say to you.... Come closer, Mathieu ... closer ... my voice is failing.... Give me your hand.... I want to be sure that you hear me."

Ropars knelt upon the sand, with one hand in that of his dying wife, and the other placed behind her, to support her.

—"You are going to stay alone," she continued. "Elsewhere, you could perhaps endure it; but here, in the midst of the ocean, it is not the life of a man, or of a Christian.... You are used to having some one keep you company ... some one to love you.... When I am gone ... another one must take my place."

—"Never!" broke in Ropars.

With her hand she silenced him.

—"Hush!" said she gently; "you must needs think this, so long as I am before your eyes ... but when I am laid in the grave, you will then feel your want.... Believe not that I would reproach you, my poor husband.... I do not wish to carry away your happiness with me in my winding sheet.... No ... no ... wherever I may be, I shall need to know that you are well cared for."

—"Enough, Geneviève!" murmured the seaman, choking with emotion.

—"Let me go on to the end," she resumed; "I have still one plea to urge.... When you take off the crape from your arm, Mathieu ... promise me to think of the dear creature who is our child ... the child of both ... and who will remain with you, to remind you of me ... choose a wife who may fill my place towards her."

—"What is it that you are asking me, and whom could I give her for a mother, after yourself?" rejoined Ropars.

—"Some one" ... Geneviève went on ... "who would not grudge me the having been chosen first ... some honest heart that would take kindly to an orphan ... who would talk to her of me ... who would teach her to love God ... and to obey you!... If you promise me that this shall be so, Mathieu ... if you promise it on your honour ... and on your salvation, I shall fall asleep, at peace, and blessing you."

Ropars made the promise, amidst sighs and groans; but this was the dying woman's last effort. After having thanked him by an embrace, she let herself sink into her husband's arms. It almost seemed as though the power of her will had slackened the steps of Death, for the sake of this final compact. Scarcely was it completed, when her sufferings recommenced. Carried back to the alcove, she died there towards the close of the day. Her last words were a prayer, in which her husband's and her daughter's names were intermingled.

On the ensuing day, the grave in which Josèphe already reposed was re- opened to receive Geneviève, for, during the past month, Death had reaped so abundantly that the barren island lacked space for his doleful harvest. Informed of what had happened, by means of the signals agreed upon, the keeper of the powder-magazine brought Francine to the edge of his rock, and the child, on her knees, uttered a prayer for her mother's spirit, at the moment the funeral ceremony was ended, across the water.

This death was the last. Like those expiatory victims who, in sacrificing themselves, were wont to appease the anger of the Gods, Geneviève seemed, in going down to the tomb, as though she closed its doors behind her. A fortnight later, and the yellow flag slid down the flag staff that over-topped the lazaretto, and those who had been quarantined, now cured, went away in the frigate's long-boat. They only left behind them, on the dreary island, a man whose hair had become perfectly white, and a child in mourning clothes.

THRICE ONLY.

I

Do not imagine that this is to be a love-story. Very few experiences furnish material for such. Rarer still is the ability to use the material, when it falls in one's way. At any rate, I make no pretension thereto.

But it sometimes happens during the earlier and more tumultuous period of a man's life, that casual occurrences take place, which do not indeed at the time immediately influence his actions or his fortunes, but which in later days may be recalled with interest. Of this sort—if I mistake not, or if I do not mar them in the telling—were my three meetings with Mary Verner. I only met her thrice.

The first time—many a year has sped away since; but it seems, if I shut my mental eye to events and feelings with which the interval has been crowded, and my bodily eye to the library table before me, as if the little scene were being enacted here, now, to-day.

Whence this power of summoning up the ghosts of long ago? Why should the comparatively recent refuse to be stamped upon the memory, and the old impressions refuse to fade? Let philosophers answer; I have no more inclination to write an essay than to tell a love-tale. My purpose I have already stated; though I omitted to mention that I write my own veritable experience—with a change of names, a studied obscurity of dates, and a very slight change otherwise.

The precise year I do not remember, nor, consequently, my own exact age; but I must have been about fourteen. George Verner, Mary's brother—poor fellow! I saw his death registered, the other day, in that odious corner of the *Times*—was my class-mate and play-mate at a school some few miles from London. He was a good-looking and good-tempered fellow, if not remarkable for his abilities. It chanced that I was—in the choice language of the time and place—"a dab at Latin verses." I helped George once in a while with his exercises; and once in a while with the mince-pies, that his mother's a cook used to send him on the sly. The first time that I saw her—Mary Verner I mean, not the cook—was on a whole holiday; George, who lived in the neighbourhood, had invited me to pass it with him. The old family coach came for us at ten o'clock, with the fat old horses and the fat old family coachman, just for all the world as you may often meet them in the story- books that are called "exceedingly natural," and as you now-a-days rarely find them in real life. Pony-phaetons, britzkas, coupés, "Croydon-baskets," and nondescript vehicles that, being neither close carriages nor open, are palmed off as both—these have superseded the full-bodied of my early recollections.

I fancy that I see her now…. You perceive that though I note the modern change in the carriage department, I recognize none such in the phraseology of our tongue. I fancy I see her now. You may, if you please, alter the wording; but that's the plain English of it.

As we drove up the sweep that led from the lodge to the front entrance of a very beautiful suburban villa, I leaned out of the window, with the curiosity natural to a boy of fourteen, on strange ground.

Mary Verner—I knew, by the family likeness, that she was George's elder sister, the moment my eye lighted on her—was trimming or watering her geraniums, in one of the recesses on either side of the porch.

"Here, Mary, here's Cuthbert *tertius*," said George, running up the steps, and pushing me before him.

"I know him; how d'ye do? I'm glad to see you," was the frank reception, spoken in a clear, round-toned, springy voice, that seemed to drop without effort out of a rose-lipped mouth well-filled with well-knit teeth. And as she spoke smilingly, she opened a pair of large brown eyes that I have since thought—for boys don't know much about the law of colours—were designed to harmonize with what we call a clear brunette complexion. Certainly, if the ballad of "The Nut Brown Mayde" be a model imitation of the antique, Mary Verner might have sat for the portrait.

But it was not so much her eyes that took hold of me, open though they did by degrees, wider and wider, until I wondered when they would cease opening; nor her coal-black hair, dressed as you may see it in the likenesses by Sir Thomas Lawrence; nor her rosy mouth; nor her even teeth; nor her figure full of grace, *svelte* as the French call it, for which we have no answering word. It was not these, or any of them. It was the carolling of her few words, so free and unconcerned in tone. If I had not met her subsequently, I might have forgotten her looks; I doubt whether her voice could have passed from me.

I need not tax my memory or my invention about the trifling though happy events of that day. It was pretty evident who was mistress of the house, though the fond and proud mother of Mary Verner had the air of a dignified and well-bred woman. Silent or talking, it was Mary who dispensed the honours, at least so far as the stranger was concerned. Probably it was the same with all comers; but this is only a surmise.

Well; the whole holiday came to an end, and we were driven back to the old school by the old coachman, our pockets full of chestnuts, and our boyish hearts full of a sense of supreme enjoyment, such we believe as, in later life, women feel after the best ball of the season, and men after a splendid whitebait dinner at Blackwall. I recollect telling the fellows in the dormitory what a jolly time we had been having, and how capitally George's pony leaped the fence on the common, round the corner, out of sight of the house. By the way, it was partly owing to that pony having engrossed so much of our time, that I had not regularly fallen in love with Mary Verner. Partly, I say, because I was further saved from this predicament by a standing devotion to my pretty cousin Rose, which the temptation had been strong enough, but not long enough to disturb. I never went to George's house again; and ere long the image of his sister was stowed away on one of the upper shelves of my memory. There it might have been smothered in dust, or even converted into it, if chance had not taken it down and given it an airing.

II

Twenty-one—what a change from fourteen! How the pulse of life beats and bounds! I was running a tilt at the pastimes, and doffing aside the cares of early manhood, when for the second time, I came across Mary Verner. Plump upon her, I would say, if I thought you would pardon the coarseness of the expression. At any rate—and to be genteel—it was unexpectedly. Twenty-one gives very few thoughts to fourteen. It may be a much longer distance thither, when one starts at seventy to go back; but it is surprising how much more quickly you get over the intermediate ground. Let that be; only I don't believe I had given a thought to Mary Verner, since the week or two that followed my first interview with her.

"Do come and dine with us on Monday," said my friend Mrs. F.; "there will be a very charming girl here, whom you would like to see."

"Positively?"

"*Sans faute!*"

"Then keep a place for me; I'll come."

I went. It was a formal dinner-party. In the drawing-room, before going to table, Mrs. F. came across to me.

"Now I'll introduce you to our belle of the evening. You may escort her down to dinner. There she is, half-hidden behind that drapery. You can't have noticed her."

"Miss Verner, let me present Mr. Cuthbert."

I should have recognized Mary Verner, as she looked up, with those widely-opening brown eyes of hers, if her name had not been mentioned. As it was, it was quite natural for me to remark that I believed I had had the pleasure of seeing Miss Verner before.

And so in a few moments we were gossipping cosily about "old times," as we, not very old people, called them.

The beautiful child had expanded into a very lovely woman, preserving still the same characteristics of person and expression. The charm of her voice was the same. You may be sure that when seated by her side, with the becoming glow of lamp-light overhead heightening, if possible, those attractions which I rather hint than attempt to describe—you may be sure, I say, that I found her very captivating.

We talked of her brother George; of the pleasant house wherein I first met her, and which was still her home; of her amiable and lady-like mother who was still living; of the old pony now gathered to his sires; of the old chestnut-trees even—in short, of all those unimportant associations, out of which, under such circumstances, one endeavours to establish a trivial and flitting but very pleasant little bond of sympathy.

I declare I was half ready to fall head over ears in love with her. And she took it all with a simple unaffected grace, that seemed to be her very nature.

But we did not have all the talk to ourselves. I had not the presumption to engross her entirely. Nor would it have been possible. She was—there is no need to go over it all again—she was Mary Verner.

Nearly opposite to us at table sat a Mr. Easton, a young barrister—young, that is professionally, for he was apparently a man of thirty or thereabouts. He would not have been singled out as a lady-killer, for he was none of your regular Adonises, such as hang by dozens, in portraiture, upon the walls of our Royal Academy Exhibitions, and lounge complacently in our Fop's Alley at the Opera. When, however, the excitement of conversation—in which he took an active and most intelligent part—developed the fine play of his features, you would have pronounced him a man who added, to a cultivated and superior mind, a look that bespoke such gift. In fact there was a manly air about him, that claimed respect, if it did not challenge attention.

About the time when I made this notable discovery, I recollected that at the moment of my introduction to Miss Verner, Mr. Easton was gossipping with her in the secluded corner half-hidden by the drapery, though he moved away, with perfect good breeding, to give place to the new-comer.

About this time, too, there began—at which end of the table, I forget—an

44

occasional play of badinage, whereof Mr. Easton was the subject. For a grave and earnest man, he seemed to receive it all in exceedingly good part. To my surprise also—to say nothing of annoyance—my fair neighbour was brought, after a while, within its scope. Neither did she—I was forced to acknowledge within myself—evince either *mauvaise honte* or sensitiveness. The truth was plain. They were engaged.

As a child's card-built house tumbles down when the table is shaken, so down went one of the prettiest little castles-in-the-air, that ever simpleton built out of cards of his own shaping.

Down it went; though I flatter myself I was too much a man of the world, to let a glimpse of its dislocated plan be apparent. Indeed, in a few seconds, I had rallied myself on my own absurdity; gulped down my disappointment; and resigned myself again to the charm that Mary Verner still shed around her, if its tint was somewhat changed. Besides, I availed myself of the sudden opportunity thus afforded, for testing the practical value of one of my favourite theories, when I was a young fellow and affected to bask in the sunshine of human nature: to wit, that, apart from serious love-making, when a woman in either married or betrothed, she has therefrom an additional feather in her social cap. So have I found it through life—always provided that the attractive and companionable qualities were otherwise in abundance. And this theory has at least given heartiness to my good wishes for my fairer acquaintances and friends. Is it not better to come to such a philosophical conclusion, than to be always envying other people's good fortune?

Shifting, therefore, my ground, I was rapidly possessed by a strong interest in Miss Verner's future welfare—much of which was undoubtedly genuine.

Delicately, and by gently leading her on, I gathered something of the story of her courtship, though I must needs confess that I cannot now call to mind a word of it. It may be of more interest to state that she was to make Mr. Easton the happiest of men, within six weeks or so of that time; and that the honey-moon was to be spent in a ramble on the Continent. Very emphatically and very sincerely did I wish her a pleasant time of it.

But the most agreeable evenings will come to a close. This one—with its revival of a boy's casual acquaintance, with its momentary castle-building, and its subsequent benevolence of feeling—this one, like all others, passed away. It did not die out, as the fag-end of a dinner-party sometimes will; it was cut short to me by the "good night!" of Mary Verner, as she took her departure, leaning on Mr. Easton's arm, in the train of an elderly female relative.

When the drawing-room door closed upon her graceful figure, I felt for a moment as though the gas had been suddenly turned off. I recollect, however, the hostess's observation, dropped to the accompaniment of a playfully malicious smile:

"Didn't I tell you, you would like my friend Mary Verner?"

"Yes," was the reply, "and I have passed a most delightful evening; but I don't think it quite fair, Mrs. F."—here there was a terrible smash of the theory —"to open the gates of Paradise, and then slam them in a poor fellow's face?"

I was to have gone, that night, to a ball in Devonshire Place, expressly to meet —Never mind; I was not in the humour for dancing or flirting. I went straight home, and to bed. I tossed about a good deal, and finally dreamed about George and the pony, and that I was climbing the old chestnut-trees. As for Mary Verner, I couldn't in my sleep conjure up her image. When I thought I had it— as is the way in dreams, you know, if you ever studied them—I couldn't get nearer to her than the plaguy old family coachman. It was only when broad awake, the next morning, that I found myself strongly impressed by this, my second meeting. But again—such is life and such is youth—the impression was soon stowed away on an upper shelf in memory's garret.

III.

Two years later; two years and two months.

Did you ever notice the marked difference between youth and old age—aye, and middle age, too—in the matter of reading newspapers? We—I speak of myself now as the writer—who are in the vanguard of the march through life, must have our *Times* or our *Chronicle*, as regularly as our morning meal. Is it, as some spitefully assert, that we grow more self-complacent as we pore over the misfortunes or the errors of our fellows; or is it, that we seek refuge from the cares and disappointments of our own lot, in a close scrutiny of that of all the world beside, with the minutiæ of which the diligent, prying, gossiping press so unceasingly plies our curiosity? It is folly, perhaps, to raise the question, since this is not the place to discuss it; though it were not far from the truth to attribute much of the pettiness of our race, in these days, to this habit of abandoning our thoughts and impulses to the guidance of journalists who trade in them.

I only mean to say that being still youthful at twenty-three, I "cared for none of these things," As for heeding who was born, or buried, or married, beyond the circle of one's own intimate connections—I should as soon have set to work to trace the pedigree of a New Zealander. Probably, I heard in due time that Mary Verner had become Mrs. Easton. Certainly I did not learn it from the usual printed record. In short, I then very seldom read newspapers at all; and this I beg you to bear in mind. What a shocking ignoramus I should be voted, if I were to say so of this present time.

That, too, was the season of darkness, ere Albert Smith was the Lecturer *par excellence*; ere Oxford and Cambridge men, returning from their "long-vacation" rambles, disputed in the daily papers their respective prowess in scaling the precipices of Monte Rosa, or discovering new pathways up Mont Blanc. How changed are we to-day! Save for the voluminous records of the Crimean war, what Mamelons and Malakoffs would the pedestrians, Smith and Jones, be now fighting over, in the *Times*!

Nevertheless, though they made less fuss about it, Englishmen were then, as now, prone to scurrying off to Switzerland in the Autumn—some in the true cockney spirit—some because they found there the most sublime of all spectacles, together with the most exhilarating exercise for the body, and relaxation of mind in its fullest sense. With myself it amounted to a passion; "Cuthbert's hobby" it was dubbed by acquaintances, who could eke out delight from Leamington and Cheltenham.

Profiting by the leisure afforded me during successive seasons, I had become tolerably familiar with the Alps; with what exquisite and inexhaustible enjoyment I am not going here to trouble you. But August had come round again. The knapsack was stitched, where it wanted mending. The Alpenstock was dragged to light, from the lumber-room. The thick-soled gaiter-boots were freshly studded with hobnails. The well-worn Swiss map was conned over once more, and a new route, leading over yet untrodden passes, was set down in the Autumnal programme.

Suddenly I changed my mind—under the influence of an hour's talk with an enthusiastic mountaineer—who had, during the previous season, explored the Pyrenees. "You may not find," said he, "quite so much grandeur; but the valleys are decidedly more picturesque, the foliage more varied, the very tints of the mountains glowing with warmer colours." Thereupon, a change of plan and passport. Behold me at Cauterets in France, instead of at Grindelwald in Switzerland!

Were my object merely to fill a certain number of pages, I might here descant at length upon the comparative beauties of the Alps and the Pyrenees—the latter having, at present, the advantage of not being done to death by tourists. But I will abstain. I will speak only of one day's adventure; the day whereon, for the third and last time, I found myself associated with Mary Verner.

Cauterets may be a pleasant place enough to those who bathe in, or imbibe for medicinal purposes, the mineral waters that have made its fame. It is finely placed too, pitched in, as it were, into a nook, with lofty peaks and fringes of fir forests over-topping its somewhat formal streets. It does not, however, offer much attraction to the connoisseur in fine scenery. One excursion alone is to be made. Its objects are the Pont d'Espagne and the Lac de Gaube. The former is a group of pine trunks bridging a cascade. The latter is a tarn at the foot of the glaciers of the Vignemale, which, you know, is one of the mountain-monarchs hereabouts.

Before proceeding further, I may mention that I am enabled to set down my reminiscences of this particular time and place, by reference to my rough notes penned on the spot, journal-wise. The little memorandum book lies under my hand, with its pages written in ink of various tints, as hotel, or cabaret, or hut furnished the material at the moment. I like to preserve these records. Such *souvenirs* are the *bonnes fortunes* of those whose travels are ended. You see that I incline to be sentimental as I draw towards the *dénouement* of my story.

Heavens and earth, how it rains in the Pyrenees! What a young deluge swept down the steep stone-guttered pavements, on the morning of the 29th of August! Still, I did not choose to devote more than one day to the neighbourhood of Cauterets; and so, having made, from my window, a few such profound observations as the one just set down, I ordered a horse and guide. The polite waiter was astonished, and protested, to the extent of two or three "*Mais Monsieur!*" The guide thought the storm would expend itself in twenty-four hours; but on my hinting that the path would not be difficult to find, without his aid, nor impracticable, on foot, he subsided, with an air of conviction, into the accustomed "*Bien, Monsieur!*"

And so we started. I had borrowed one of the long, thick, hooded Spanish cloaks, commonly used in that region which borders on Spain; and a very effectual protection it was against the steady down-pouring of the rain. But what is perfect in this world? A German counterpane, on a summer's night, is not more oppressive than was this excellent protection from the wet.

Handing, then, the heavy encumbrance to the guide, I was drenched to the skin in about two minutes. This was a comfort. It settled the point. I dislike uncertainty. I could be at my ease, and look about. Remember it was yet August.

And the Val de Jéret, up which I was riding, was so grandly gloomy; the state of the weather excluding all but close views! My note-book thus speaks of it, the writer never dreaming that his impressions would be told to the readers of a newspaper, with many of whom Niagara and Montmorenci are familiar sights: "The valley presents a succession of splendid waterfalls; and, singularly enough, as your route lies upwards, they increase in size and beauty, from the Mahourat, the first, to the Pont d'Espagne, the last and most celebrated. The three intervening, that are dignified with names, are the Cérizet, the Boussé, and the Pas de l'Ours. Besides these, there are an infinity of smaller falls, the whole course of the Gave (or torrent) de Marcadaou—along which the path lies—boiling over broken masses of rock. The eye is charmed by endless variety, amid perpetual repetition. The deluge of rain, which covered the lofty rocks on each side of the defile with clouds, had gloriously swollen the turbulent waters. I know of nothing in natural scenery —thus the manuscript rather enthusiastically proceeds—that impresses one so forcibly as a cascade of large dimensions. By large I mean broad, not lofty. The effect is apt to diminish, with vast height. These, in the Val de Jéret, I found absolutely bewitching; for is it not a sort of infatuation, by which we are beguiled into drawing nearer and nearer, until you almost touch the foaming sheets as they flurry past, and are yourself driven back, for your pains, half blind and breathless? One fine waterfall would be enough to digest in a day. During these two or three hours, I had a very feast of them."

If I extract this somewhat rhapsodical passage, it is to show that my inward man was not dampened, by the dampening process externally applied. On the contrary, I am disposed to be jubilant, almost defiant, in proportion to the fury of the storm; that is to say when no serious personal inconvenience is caused by stress of weather. In a mountain region too, above all others, clouds play so great a part in the combination of fine effects, that I have many times fairly welcomed a tempestuous spell.

Thus from the Pont d'Espagne I continued my ride an hour or so further, in order to reach the Lac de Gaube, knowing perfectly well that the chances were a hundred to one against my getting a glimpse of the glaciers of the Vignemale, at whose feet this small sheet of water is imbedded. Small it may well be termed, for it is not quite three miles in circumference, though the largest lake in the Pyrenees.

On the rocky shore where the rough pathway terminates, stands, or stood at the period of which I write, a solitary hut. There, during the short summer season, might be found a family who earned a scanty subsistence, by catching the lake trout and serving them up to chance travellers; by rowing, in the solitary punt, any one who cared to paddle about the dark waters; or by escorting any still more adventurous stranger desirous of exploring the glaciers above-named, or ascending the lower heights of the Vignemale.

Stepping up to the door of this cabin, I entered into conversation with its chief occupant, who probably combined in his own person the various offices of restaurateur, fisherman, muleteer, guide, and smuggler. Possibly I libel him in the last respect; but along that frontier of France and Spain, it is rare to find a mountaineer guiltless of the contraband trade.

A visitor on such a day was a welcome sight to the poor fellow, who was eloquent in regrets that *his* mountain and *his* glaciers and *his* other local points of interest were all wrapped in the impenetrable mist. He seemed, I remember now, to care more about it than I did; for I had revelled in the exhibition of cascades, and was rather tickled at the notion of having come up to this lone and savage spot, where nothing whatever was to be seen.

If a spirit had whispered me, that the moment of my third *rencontre* was close at hand, I should have smiled incredulously.

The fog lifted. I could see to a distance of half a dozen yards.

"What's that?"

"If Monsieur will give himself the trouble of walking up to it, he will see."

It was on a jutting promontory of rock, close at hand. A small enclosure was railed in. It held what was obviously a monumental tablet, in white marble, but discoloured by exposure.

"A favourite poodle, perhaps, of the Duchesse de Berri—or one of our eccentric Englishmen doing honour to a Pyrenean bear!" Such I thought it might be, as I carelessly lounged up to it, and stooped to read the inscription.

It was in French and English. I took no copy of the words. But it was placed there in memory of Mr. and Mrs. Easton, drowned in the lake, within one month of their marriage, on the 20th of September, 18—! The facts were simply stated. I wish the record of them had been placed a little further off from the rendezvous of the thoughtless and light-hearted.

This was the last of my associations with her. But it would not interest the reader, to be told with what feelings of surprise and sorrow I thus learned the close of a career, which bid so fair for happiness and usefulness. Poor Mary Verner!

Before setting-off on my return to Cauterets, I heard, from the lips of the man with whom I had been conversing, the sad particulars of this harrowing event. Never could the common phrase, that speaks of "painful curiosity," have been more applicable than it was in my case, as I stood and listened to him. Poor fellow; he had been an eye-witness. He saw my emotion. "Monsieur knew the young couple?"—thus did he break the thread of his little narrative, more than once.

I cannot pretend to set down his words. This is the substance of what he told me.

The season was nearly over. The weather was splendidly fine, but very cold.

Travellers were scarcely expected; when on that brilliant September morning, up rode the bride and bridegroom. After resting awhile, they took the single skiff that was there, Mr. Easton offering to row his wife across the lake, to which she very reluctantly assented. I recollect the narrator dwelling on this fact.

The shore shelves off very rapidly. The water, in some parts, reaches to the depth of three or four hundred feet. At all times it is of marvellous clearness —as I observed myself—and, except during the heats of summer, so piercingly cold, as to be altogether unbearable to the swimmer.

My informant helped them into the boat. Mr. Easton was evidently used to the handling of oars. The tragedy was immediately—perhaps one should say, ostensibly—caused by those two qualities of the water of the Lac de Gaube, to which I have just alluded—its clearness and its coldness.

The boat was at some considerable distance from the shore. The boatman was watching them. Suddenly, Mr. Easton paused in his rowing. He and his wife looked over the side, as though guessing at the depth. Mr. Easton then stood up, and plunged one oar downwards into the water, with the confident action of a man who is certain that he shall touch the bottom. The transparency had deceived him. His oar met no resistance; and he himself plunged heavily overboard. Such at least was the impression of the boatman on land; and he could scarcely be mistaken.

So far as he could see, Mr. Easton did not rise to the surface. The cold numbed him, and he sunk, not to rise again. The bereaved wife stood upright for a moment in the boat, gazing on the water that had swallowed up her husband before her eyes. Then she too was seen to be in it; but not one of the two or three, who witnessed the fearful sight, could tell whether she threw herself in, or whether she fell in, senseless. That secret will never be solved; and what matters it to us, though the manner of the widowed wife's death was so remarkable, that I cannot refrain from mentioning it? In talking it over, they agreed that she did not sink at all. As she fell, the water inflated her dress, and she was buoyed-up, floating; though there was no sign of life or movement on her part, observable to the agonized spectators. After a time—I forget whether it was half an hour, or half a day—the remains of what once was loved as Mary Verner were wafted tranquilly to the shore. Assistance also having been procured, Mr. Easton's body was dragged-up from the bottom of the lake. One grave in a church-yard in Essex now holds the coffins of the ill- fated pair.

And was there no effort at rescue? Could nothing be done? This idea will have crossed the reader's mind. It suggested many questions to me, with which I plied the boatman, who seemed to feel keenly in them the bitterness of unintended reproach. But his explanation—grievous as it was—was satisfactory. There was no boat, no raft, no means of reaching the spot. "Two of us," said he, "plunged up to our necks into the water, in the irrepressible desire to swim out to them; though we knew that it was certain death to go beyond our depth. Besides, Monsieur," he added with touching simplicity, "I can't help fancying that the poor lady was dead before she fell out of the boat. Monsieur knew her; doesn't he think that her heart was already broken?"

"God help her, and all of us, my brave friend; I have not the smallest doubt of it!"

TOSSING UP FOR A HUSBAND.

From the French of Vicomte Ponson de Terrail.

I.

The Marchioness was at her toilet. Florine and Aspasia, her two ladies'- maids, were busy powdering, as it were with hoar-frost, the bewitching widow.

She was a widow, this Marchioness, a widow of twenty-three; and wealthy, as very few persons were any longer at the court of Louis XV., her godfather.

Three-and-twenty years earlier, his Majesty had held her at the baptismal font of the chapel at Marly, and had settled upon her an income of a hundred thousand livres, by way of proving to her father, the Baron Fontevrault, who had saved his life in the battle of Fontenoy, that kings can be grateful, whatever people choose to say to the contrary.

The Marchioness then was a widow. She resided during the summer, in a charming little chateau, situated half-way up the slope overhanging the water, on the road from Bougival to Saint Germain. Madame Dubarry's estate adjoined hers; and on opening her eyes she could see, without rising, the white gableends and the white-spreading chestnut-trees of Luciennes, perched upon the heights. On this particular day—it was noon—the Marchioness, whilst her attendants dressed her hair and arranged her head-dress with the most exquisite taste, gravely employed herself in tossing up, alternately, a couple of fine oranges, which crossed each other in the air, and then dropped into the white and delicate hand that caught them in their fall.

This sleight-of-hand—which the Marchioness interrupted at times whilst she adjusted a beauty-spot on her lip, or cast an impatient glance on the crystal clock that told how time was running away with the fair widow's precious moments—had lasted for ten minutes, when the folding-doors were thrown open, and a valet, such as one sees now only on the stage announced with pompous voice—"The King!"

Apparently, the Marchioness was accustomed to such visits, for she but half rose from her seat, as she saluted with her most gracious smile the personage who entered.

It was indeed Louis XV. himself—Louis XV. at sixty-five; but robust, upright, with smiling lip and beaming eye, and jauntily clad in a close-fitting, pearl-grey hunting-suit, that became him to perfection. He carried under his arm a handsome fowling-piece, inlaid with mother-of-pearl; a small pouch, intended for ammunition alone, hung over his shoulder.

The King had come from Luciennes, almost alone, that is but with a Captain of the Guard, the old Marshal de Richelieu, and a single Equerry on foot. He had been amusing himself with quail-shooting, loading his own gun, as was the fashion with his ancestors, the later Valois and the earlier Bourbons. His grandsire, Henry IV., could not have been less ceremonious.

But a shower of hail had surprised him; and his Majesty had no relish for it. He pretended that the fire of an enemy's battery was less disagreeable than those drops of water, so small and so hard, that wet him through, and reminded him of his twinges of rheumatism.

Fortunately, he was but a few steps from the gateway of the chateau, when the shower commenced. He had come therefore to take shelter with his god-daughter, having dismissed his suite, and only keeping with him a magnificent pointer, whose genealogy was fully established by the Duc de Richelieu, and traced back, with a few slips in orthography, directly to Nisus, that celebrated greyhound, given by Charles IX. to his friend Ronsard, the poet.

"Good morning, Marchioness," said the King, as he entered, putting down his fowling-piece in a corner. "I have come to ask your hospitality. We were caught in a shower at your gate—Richelieu and I. I have packed off Richelieu."

"Ah, Sire, that wasn't very kind of you."

"Hush!" replied the King, in a good-humored tone. "It's only mid-day; and if the Marshal had forced his way in here at so early an hour, he would have bragged of it every where, this very evening. He is very apt to compromise one, and he is a great coxcomb too, the old Duke. But don't put yourself out of the way, Marchioness. Let Aspasia finish this becoming pile of your head-dress, and Florine spread out with her silver knife the scented powder that blends so well with the lilies and the roses of your bewitching face…. Why, Marchioness, you are so pretty, one could eat you up!"

"You think me so, Sire?"

"I tell you so every day. Oh, what fine oranges!"

And the King seated himself upon the roomy sofa, by the side of the Marchioness, whose rosy finger-tips he kissed with an infinity of grace. Then taking up one of the oranges that he had admired, he proceeded leisurely to examine it.

"But," said he at length, "what are oranges doing by the side of your Chinese powder-box and your scent bottles? Is there any connection between this fruit and the maintenance—easy as it is, Marchioness—of your charms?"

"These oranges," replied the lady, gravely, "fulfilled just now, Sire, the functions of destiny."

The King opened wide his eyes, and stroked the long ears of his dog, by way of giving the Marchioness time to explain her meaning.

"It was the Countess who gave them to me," she continued.

"Madame Dubarry?"

"Exactly so, Sire."

"A trumpery gift, it seems to me, Marchioness."

"I hold it, on the contrary, to be an important one; since I repeat to your Majesty, that these oranges decide my fate."

"I give it up," said the King.

"Imagine, Sire; yesterday I found the Countess occupied in tossing her oranges up and down, in this way." And the Marchioness recommenced her game with a skill that cannot be described.

"I see," said the King; "she accompanied this singular amusement with the words, 'Up, Choiseul! up, Praslin!' and, on my word, I can fancy how the pair jumped."

"Precisely so, Sire."

"And do you dabble in politics, Marchioness? Have you a fancy for uniting with the Countess, just to mortify my poor ministers?"

"By no means, Sire; for, in place of Monsieur de Choiseul and the Duc de Praslin, I was saying to myself, just now, 'Up, Menneval! up, Beaugency!'"

"Ay, ay," returned the King; "and why the deuce would you have them jumping, those two good-looking gentlemen—Monsieur de Menneval, who is a Croesus, and Monsieur de Beaugency, who is a statesman, and dances the minuet to perfection?"

"I'll tell you," said the dame. "You know, Sire, that Monsieur de Menneval is an accomplished gentleman, a handsome man, a gallant cavalier, an indefatigable dancer, witty as Monsieur Arouet, and longing for nothing so much as to live in the country, on his estate in Touraine, on the banks of the Loire, with the woman whom he loves or will love, far from the court, from grandeur, and from turmoil."

"And, on my life, he's in the right of it," quoth the King. "One does become so wearied at court."

"Aye, and no," rejoined the widow as she put on her last beauty-spot.... "Nor are you unaware, Sire, that Monsieur de Beaugency is one of the most brilliant courtiers of Marly and Versailles; ambitious, burning with zeal for the service of your Majesty; as brave as Monsieur de Menneval, and capable of going to the end of the earth … with the title of Ambassador of the King of France."

"I know that," chimed in Louis XV., with a laugh. "But, alas, I have more ambassadors than embassies. My ante-chambers overflow every morning."

"Now," continued the Marchioness, "I have been a widow … these two years past."

"A long time, there's no denying."

"Ah," sighed she, "there's no need to tell me so, Sire. But Monsieur de Menneval loves me … at least he says so, and I am easilypersuaded."

"Very well; then marry Monsieur deMenneval."

"I have thought of it, Sire; and, in truth, I might do much worse. I should like well enough to live in the country, under the willow-trees, on the borders of the river, with a husband, fond, yielding, loving, who would detest the philosophers and set some little value on the poets. When no external noises disturb the honey-moon, that month, Sire, may be indefinitely prolonged. In the country, you know, one never hears a noise."

"Unless it be the north-wind moaning in the corridor, and the rain pattering on the window-panes." And the King shivered slightly on his sofa.

"But," added the dame, "Monsieur de Beaugency loves me equally well."

"Ah, ah! the ambitious man!"

"Ambition does not shut out love, Sire. Monsieur de Beaugency is a Marquis; he is twenty-five; he is ambitious—I should like a husband vastly who was longing to reach high offices of state. Greatness has its own particular merit."

"Then marry Monsieur de Beaugency."

"I have thought of that, also; but this poor Monsieur de Menneval."…

"Very good," exclaimed the King, laughing: "now I see to what purpose the oranges are destined. Monsieur de Menneval pleases you; Monsieur de Beaugency would suit you just as well; and since one can't have more than one husband, you make them each jump in turn."

"Just so, Sire. But observe whathappens."

"Ah, what does happen?"

"That, unwilling and unable to play unfairly, I take equal pains to catch the two oranges as they come down; and that I catch them both, each time."

"Well, are you willing that I should take part in your game?"

"You, Sire? Ah, what a joke that would be!"

"I am very clumsy, Marchioness. To a certainty, in less than three minutes Beaugency and Menneval, will be rolling on the floor."

"Ah!" exclaimed the lady; "and if you have any preference for one or the other?"

"No; we'll do better. Look, I take the two oranges … you mark them carefully —or, better still, you stick into one of them one of these toilet pins, making up your own mind which of the two is to represent Monsieur de Beaugency, and leaving me, on that point, entirely in the dark. If Monsieur de Beaugency touches the floor, you shall marry his rival; if it happen just otherwise, you shall resign yourself to become an ambassadress."

"Excellent! Now, Sire, let's see the result."

The King took the two oranges and plied shuttle with them above his head. But at the third pass, the two rolled down upon the embroidered carpet, and the Marchioness broke out into a merry fit of laughter.

"I foresaw as much," exclaimed his Majesty. "What a clumsy fellow I am!"

"And we more puzzled than ever, Sire?"

"So we are, Marchioness; but the best thing we can do, is to slice the oranges, sugar them well, and season them with a dash of West India rum. Then you can beg me to taste them, and offer me some of those preserved cherries and peaches that you put up just as nicely as my daughter Adelaide."

"And Monsieur de Menneval? and Monsieur de Beaugency?" said the Marchioness, in piteous accents. "How is the question to be settled?"

Louis XV. began to cogitate.

"Are you quite sure," said he, "that both of them are in love with you?"

"Probably so," returned she, with a little coquettish smile, sent back to her from the mirror opposite.

"And their love is equally strong?"

"I trust so, Sire."

"And I don't believe a word of it."

"Ah!" said the Marchioness, "but that is, in truth, a most terrible supposition. Besides, Sire, they are on their way hither."

"Both of them?"

"One after the other: the Marquis at one o'clock precisely; the Baron at two. I promised them my decision to-morrow, on condition that they would pay me a final visit to-day."

As the Marchioness finished, the valet, who had announced the King, came to inform his mistress, that Monsieur de Beaugency was in the drawing-room, and solicited the favour of admission to pay his respects.

"Capital!" said Louis XV., smiling as though he were eighteen; "show Monsieur de Beaugency in. Marchioness, you will receive him, and tell him the price that you set upon your hand."

"And what is the price, Sire?"

"You must give him the choice—either to renounce you, or to consent to send in to me his resignation of his appointments, in order that he may go and bury himself with his wife on his estate of Courlac, in Poitou, there to live the life of a country gentleman."

"And then, Sire?"

"You will allow him a couple of hours for reflection, and so dismiss him."

"And in the end?"

"The rest is my concern." And the King got up, taking his dog and his gun, and concealed himself behind a screen, drawing also a curtain, that he might be completely hidden.

"What is your intention, Sire?" asked the Marchioness.

"I conceal myself like the kings of Persia, from the eyes of my subjects," replied Louis XV. "Hush, Marchioness."

A few moments later, and Monsieur de Beaugency entered the room.

II.

The Marquis was a charming cavalier; tall, slight, with a moustache black and curling upwards, an eye sparkling and intelligent, a Roman nose, an Austrian lip, a firm step, a noble and imposing presence.

The Marchioness blushed slightly, at sight of him, but offered him her hand to kiss; and as she begged him by a gesture to be seated, thus inwardly took counsel with herself.

"Decidedly, I believe that the test is useless; it is Monsieur de Beaugency whom I love. How proud shall I be to lean upon his arm at the court-fêtes! With what delight shall I keep long watches in the cabinet of his Excellency the Ambassador, whilst he is busy with his Majesty's affairs!"

But after this "aside," the Marchioness resumed her gracious and coquettish air; as though the woman comprehended the mission of refined gallantry which was reserved for her seductive and delicate epoch by an indulgent Providence, that laid by its anger and its evil days for the subsequent reign.

"Marchioness," said Monsieur de Beaugency, as he held in his hands the rosy fingers of the lovely widow, "it is fully a week since you received me!"

"A week? why, you were here yesterday!"

"Then I must have counted the hours for ages."

"A compliment which may be found in one of the younger Crebillon's books!"

"You are hard upon me, Marchioness."

"Perhaps so, … it comes naturally … I am tired."

"Ah, Marchioness! Heaven knows that I would make of your existence one never-ending fête!"

"That would, at least, be wearisome."

"Say a word, Madam, one single word, and my fortune, my future prospects, my ambition!"—

"You are still then as ambitious as ever?"

"More than ever, since I have been in love with you."

"Is that necessary?"

"Beyond a doubt. Ambition—what is it but honours, wealth, the envious looks of impotent rivals, the admiration of the crowd, the favour of monarchs?… And is not one's love unanswerably and most triumphantly proved, in laying all this at the feet of the woman whom one adores?"

"You may be right."

"I may be right, Marchioness! Listen to me, my fair lady-love."

"I am all attention, sir."

"Between us, who are well-born, and consort not with plebeians, that vulgar and sentimental sort of love, which is painted by those who write books for your mantuamakers and chambermaids, would be in exceedingly bad taste. It would be but slighting love and making no account of its enjoyments, were we to go and bury it in some obscure corner of the Provinces, or of Paris— we, who belong to Versailles—living away there with it, in monotonous solitude and unchanging contemplation!"

"Ah!" said the Marchioness, "you think so?"

"Tell me, rather, of fêtes that dazzle one with lights, with noise, with smiles, with wit, through which one glides intoxicated, with the fair conquest in triumph on one's arm … why hide one's happiness, in place of parading it? The jealousy of the world does but increase, and cannot diminish it. My uncle, the Cardinal, stands well at court. He has the King's ear, and better still, the Countess's. He will, ere long, procure me one of the Northern embassies. Cannot you fancy yourself Madame the Ambassadress, treading the platform of a drawing-room, as royalty with royalty, with the highest nobility of a kingdom—having the men at your feet, and the women on lower seats around you, whilst you yourself are occupant of a throne, and wield a sceptre?"

And as Monsieur de Beaugency warmed with his own eloquence, he gently slid from his seat to the knees of the Marchioness, whose hand he covered with kisses.

She listened to him, with a smile on her lips, and then abruptly said to him:

"Rise, sir, and hear me in turn. Are you in truth sincerely attached to me?"

"With my whole soul, Marchioness!"

"Are you prepared to make every sacrifice?"

"Every one, Madam."

"That is fortunate indeed; for to be prepared for all, is to accomplish one, without the slightest difficulty; and it is but a single one that I require."

"Oh, speak! Must a throne be conquered?"

"By no means, sir. You must only call to mind that you own a fine chateau in Poitou."

"Pooh!" said Monsieur de Beaugency, "a shed."

"Every man's house is his castle," replied the widow. "And having called it to mind, you need only order post-horses."

"For what purpose?"

"To carry me off to Courlac. It is there that your almoner shall unite us, in the chapel, in presence of your domestics and your vassals, our only witnesses."

"A singular whim, Marchioness; but I submit to it."

"Very well. We will set out this evening…. Ah! I forgot."

"What, further?"

"Before starting, you will send in your resignation to the King."

Monsieur de Beaugency almost bounded from his seat.

"Do you dream of that, Marchioness?"

"Assuredly. You will not, at Courlac, be able to perform your duties at court."

"And on returning?"

"We will not return."

"We will—not—return!" slowly ejaculated Monsieur de Beaugency. "Where then shall we proceed?"

"Nowhere. We will remain at Courlac."

"All the winter?"

"And all the summer. I count upon settling myself there, after our marriage. I have a horror of the court. I do not like the turmoil. Grandeur wearies me…. I look forward only to a simple and charming country life, to the tranquil and happy existence of the forgotten lady of the castle…. What matters it to you? You were ambitious for my love's sake. I care but little for ambition; you ought to care for it still less, since you are in love with me."

"But, Marchioness—"

"Hush! it's a bargain…. Still, for form's sake, I give you one hour to reflect. There, pass out that way; go into the winter drawing-room that you will find at the end of the gallery, and send me your answer upon a leaf of your tablets. I am about to complete my toilet, which I left unfinished, to receive you."

And the Marchioness opened a door, bowed Monsieur de Beaugency into the corridor, and closed the door upon him.

"Marchioness," cried the King, from his hiding place and through the screen, "you will offer Monsieur de Menneval the embassy to Prussia, which I promise you for him."

"And you will not emerge from your retreat?"

"Certainly not, Madame; it is far more amusing to remain behind the scenes.

One hears all, laughs at one's ease, and is not troubled with saying any thing."

It struck two. Monsieur de Menneval was announced. His Majesty remained snug, and shammed dead.

III.

Monsieur de Menneval was, at all points, a cavalier who yielded nothing to his rival, Monsieur de Beaugency. He was fair. He had a blue eye, a broad forehead, a mouth that wore a dreamy expression, and that somewhat pensive air which became so well the Troubadours of France in the olden time.

We cannot say whether Monsieur de Menneval had perpetrated verse; but he loved the poets, the arts, the quiet of the fields, the sunsets, the rosy dawn, the breeze sighing through the foliage, the low and mysterious tones of a harp, sounding at eve from the light bark shooting over the blue waters of the Loire —all things in short that harmonize with that melodious concert of the heart, which passes by the name of love.

He was timid, but he passionately loved the beautiful widow; and his dearest dream was of passing his whole life at her feet, in well chosen retirement, far from those envious lookers-on who are ever ready to fling their sarcasms on quiet happiness, and who dissemble their envy under cloak of a philosophic scepticism.

He trembled, as he entered the Marchioness's boudoir. He remained standing before her, and blushed as he kissed her hand. At length, encouraged by a smile, emboldened by the solemnity of this coveted interview, he spoke to her of his love, with a poetic simplicity and an unpremeditated warmth of heart— the genuine enthusiasm of a priest, who has faith in the object of his adoration.

And as he spoke, the Marchioness sighed, and said within herself:

"He is right. Love is happiness. Love is to be two indeed, but one at the same time; and to be free from those importunate intermeddlers, the indifference or the mocking attention of the world."

She remembered, however, the advice of the King, and thus addressed the Baron:

"What will you indeed do, in order to convince me of your affection?"

"All that man can do."

The Baron was less bold than Monsieur de Beaugency, who had talked of conquering a throne. He was probably more sincere.

"I am ambitious," said the widow.

"Ah!" replied Monsieur de Menneval, sorrowfully.

"And I would that the man, whom I marry, should aspire to every thing, and achieve every thing."

"I will try so to do, if you wish it."

"Listen; I give you an hour to reflect. I am, you know, the King's god-daughter. I have begged of him an embassy for you."

"Ah!" said Monsieur de Menneval, with indifference.

"He has granted my request. If you love me, you will accept the offer. We will be married this evening, and your Excellency the Ambassador to Prussia will set off for Berlin immediately after the nuptials. Reflect; I grant you an hour."

"It is useless," answered Monsieur de Menneval; "I have no need of reflection, for I love you. Your wishes are my orders: to obey you is my only desire. I accept the embassy."

"Never mind!" said she, trembling with joy and blushing deeply. "Pass into the room, wherein you were just now waiting. I must complete my toilet, and I shall then be at your service. I will summon you."

The Marchioness handed out the Baron by the right-hand door, as she had handed out the Marquis by the left; and then said to herself:

"I shall be prettily embarrassed, if Monsieur de Beaugency should consent to end his days at Courlac!"

Thereupon, the King removed the screen and reappeared.

His Majesty stepped quietly to the round table, whereupon he had replaced the oranges, and took up one of them.

"Ah!" exclaimed the Marchioness, "I perceive, Sire, that you foresee the difficulty that is about to spring up, and go back accordingly to the oranges, in order to settle it."

As his sole reply, Louis XV. took a small ivory handled pen-knife from his waistcoat pocket, made an incision in the rind of the orange, peeled it off very neatly, divided the fruit into two parts, and offered one to the astonished Marchioness.

"But, Sire, what are you doing?" was her eager inquiry.

"You see that I am eating the orange."

"But—"

"It was of no manner of use to us."

"You have decided then?"

"Unquestionably. Monsieur de Menneval loves you better than Monsieur de Beaugency."

"That is not quite certain yet; let us wait."

"Look," said the King, pointing to the valet, who entered with a note from the Marquis, "You'll soon see."

The widow opened the note, and read:

"Madam, I love you—Heaven is my witness; and to give you up is the most cruel of sacrifices. But I am a gentleman. A gentleman belongs to the King. My life, my blood are his. I cannot, without forfeit of my loyalty, abandon his service———."

"Et cetera," chimed in the King, "as was observed by the Abbé Fleury, my tutor. Marchioness, call in Monsieur de Menneval."

Monsieur de Menneval entered, and was greatly troubled to see the King in the widow's boudoir.

"Baron," said his Majesty, "Monsieur de Beaugency was deeply in love with the Marchioness; but he was more deeply still in love—since he would not renounce it, to please her—with the embassy to Prussia. And you, you love the Marchioness so much better than you love me, that you would only enter my service for her sake. This leads me to believe that you would be but a lukewarm public servant, and that Monsieur de Beaugency will make an excellent ambassador. He will start for Berlin this evening; and you shall marry the Marchioness. I will be present at the ceremony."

"Marchioness," whispered Louis XV. in the ear of his god-daughter, "true love is that which does not shrink from a sacrifice."

And the King peeled the second orange and eat it, as he placed the hand of the widow in that of the Baron.

"I have been making three persons happy: the Marchioness, whose indecision I have relieved; the Baron, who shall marry her; and Monsieur do Beaugency, who will perchance prove a sorry ambassador. In all this, I have only neglected my own interests, for I have been eating the oranges without sugar.... And yet they pretend to say that I am a selfish Monarch?"

THE MISSING MARINERS,

A DREAM OF THE ARCTIC SEAS.

This fanciful sketch was written and published, before the fate of Sir
John Franklin and his Discovery Ships was known.

There was not a curtain of any kind over the window.

Now, there are few things that I dislike more than this total want of privacy in
a bed-room. Opposite to a dead wall at a foot's distance, so that none but bogies
could peer within, or looking out through a port-hole over the lonely sea, I
confess to an almost old-maidenish particularity in this respect. Failing,
therefore, in sundry efforts to substitute a great coat for a curtain, or even to
delude myself into a sense of seclusion, by planting an open umbrella upon a
chair before the window, I finally abandoned my efforts, determined to brazen
it out, blew out my light, and tumbled into bed, not in the best of humours.

You remember, perhaps, the bitter cold night and the flurry of a snow storm,
that came abruptly upon us, a few weeks since. That was the time of which I
write—the place was a country village. And what a freezing night it was! The
east wind blew gustily and drearily. It was moonlight, but dull and grey; and
as I lay in bed, without raising my head from the starveling bolster vainly eked
out by a meagre carpet bag, I could see a single pine tree, on a steep bank right
opposite my window, nodding, and bowing at me by fits and by starts, as
though the capricious spirit of the night wind had bid it mock me. How I longed
for the sight of a chimney-pot!

There was no snow yet; but I listened to the rush of each driving blast, and
shrunk, huddling under the clothes, from the chill it sent through me, as its
keen edges forced their way through the crevices of the roof over my head. At
length, and after much tumbling and tossing, I fell asleep—or believed that I
did so; and presently I awoke again—or so it seemed to me. What was sleeping,
and what was waking, I scarcely knew, that night.

Suddenly, there, between us—between myself, I mean, and the white, shining
hill-side—came an object, undefined in form but palpable in substance,
waving gently to and fro, passing and repassing before the window, and at last
appearing almost to touch it. Finally it became stationary there, yet still
undulating with that soft tremulous motion which you may have noticed in the
humming-bird, when, poised upon his delicate wings, he darts his slender
tongue into the petals of a favourite flower. "What in the world is it?" I
exclaimed; and had just fancied that I could see a few slight cords reaching

65

from it upwards, above the upper edge of the window, when I distinctly heard a rap upon the pane, and sprung from my bed, in wonderment, but not in fear. The glass melted away—frame-work to the casement there was none—I passed outwards, unconscious how or wherefore. I was seated, warmly and comfortably seated, springing aloft into the moonlit and starry sky.

Then I knew that it was a balloon. It rose at the instant, and sped rapidly through the air. The wind was strong, but blowing a steady gale; not in gusts now, as it had been. And I felt that it was from the south, for it was soft and balmy; and I knew that I was driving towards the Polar star, for I saw it; and saw it growing larger and more luminous.

Then my spirit yearned after the missing Mariners; and I prayed Heaven that I might be on my way to find them.

On we sped; but I was conscious, though the southerly gales were wafting me to the frozen regions of the North, that there was a spirit beneath or behind me, guiding the tiny car in which I was borne. I felt that he was there, though I strove in vain to detect his presence. Slily did I glance over my shoulder, abruptly did I turn my head, cautiously did I crane over the edge—I could not see him. I felt him directing my looks to what I beheld, shaping my thoughts whitherward they went; but it pleased him to remain invisible.

It was yet night. Many rivers did we cross in our progress, some looking inky-black as they flowed between snowy banks, others dimly made out, and lost in the one unvaried tone. Lakes were there, too, and cities sparcely scattered. The latter were mostly slumbering in the same quiet as the former; but ascending from one I heard the alarm of a bell, and glanced downwards at a herd of figures who seemed to be fussing and fuming around a fire.

And now, for a moment, I knew that I was dreaming; and oh, grievous disappointment, I half awoke to a consciousness that the vision was slipping away from me. How I clutched at it! how I hugged it, and refused to have a word to say to my senses! Did you never try this plan and succeed in it? If not, I would not give a fig for your dreams.

But I caught up the thread of mine. Bravo! It was a narrow escape, though. They told me, next day, that there had been a false alarm of fire in the village, during the night. I would have been roasted alive, rather than not have dreamed out my dream.

Day-light, and early summer, and we were hovering over the icy land and icy sea, scarcely now distinguishable, one from other. Nor can I, indeed, describe much of what I saw; for methought, that we were driving hither and thither, not only in the dreary realm of the Frost-king, but up, and down, and athwart the ordinary current of times and seasons. So was there much confusion. Anon it was that awful Winter, whose cold will eat, like red-hot iron, into the unguarded flesh, or more fatal still, will palm off Death upon his victim under the alluring disguise of Slumber—Winter, with his terrible silence, more fearful than the roar of his fiercest hurricanes—Winter, with his blinding mantle of unbroken white, and his snowdrifts wherein cities might be engulphed—Winter, with his one redeeming beauty, one attendant goddess, one Aurora, the Borealis, whose coruscations were so marvellous to behold, so changeful, so grand, so brilliant, that I smiled in looking on them, to think that ever human skill had fabricated fire-works, and that their display could throw spectators into ecstacies.

And anon it was the Arctic summer—and the blue waters peeped at intervals between giant pyramids of ice—pyramids, and pinnacles, and turrets, and all shapely and all shapeless masses. And these were floating in the sunlight— some majestically sailing through the ever opening spaces, coming never in contact with their fellows—others jarring, and crashing, and splintering into a thousand fragments, as the upheaving waves compelled them perilously to embrace each other; and their greeting was as the roar of thunder-storms. And uncouth walrusses were playing their clumsy antics on detached fragments of the ice, and the seal was basking in the sun, and the huge whale was spouting, and the seagull was skimming the surface of the loosened deep, dipping therein the tips of his wings, as though to assure himself that it was indeed liquid. Landward, too—for there was land, also, beneath us—I seemed to see the scanty blades of a dwarfish vegetation thrusting themselves pertinaciously through the snow; and anon the garb of the earth seemed changing from one universal white, to varied hues of brown and green.

Those things and other such, rare and beautiful, were visible to the bodily eye; but the eye of my mind was not therewith content. It strained its utmost, but saw not what it longed for; and my voice broke out in bitterness, "Oh, the ships and the men, the men and the ships, the good Sir John and his daring crews!"

Then I was conscious that my attendant spirit impelled the balloon in a direction hitherto unexplored, and lo! there beneath us was a ship—a ship, one of the objects of my search!

A ship! and my heart bounded within me at the first glimpse I caught of it. But ah! how the blood curdled in my veins, when, at the next moment, I saw that the ship had not, and could not have occupants. Poor, ill-fated, ill-treated vessel; never surely did typhoon or whirlwind so displace thee from thy proper bearings. The troubled waters of the Atlantic or the Caribbean Sea might indeed have reared thee upwards, and plunged thee downwards, and made thee reel to and fro, like a drunkard; but it was alone the frozen waters of the Arctic, that could have forced thee into this unnatural position, and then cruelly nailed thee there, to rot into decay.

Ay, stout ship *Erebus* or *Terror*—I wot not which—there wert thou lying, or rather there didst thou stand upright, thy bows grovelling in the ice, thy stern uplifted high in air, thy keel propped up against a sheer precipice of ice, thy bowsprit shivered into splinters, thy masts and yards, and tackle, fallen all, and tangled in most inextricable confusion. One stick alone remained set out horizontally from the deck. From it drooped the tattered remnant of a flag; it was the blood-red standard of England!

As the balloon glided downwards towards the wreck, I could have peered into the after-cabin windows; but a single glance had already satisfied me that no living being would be found on board. I have said that my blood curdled in my veins. Turning hastily with a sudden movement of indignation, I obtained a moment's glance at my guide—his form was shadowy; but by his hideous features I recognized him as Despair, and felt that he and I were one.

But ho, a pleasant change! Down we floated, till my tiny car was almost on a level with the vessel's bows; and there—oh, joy of joys—were signs, palpable and undoubted, that the crew had fared better than their ship—that they had escaped, and were gone, and had carried what they pleased away with them. At one view I comprehended this—I read it in the aperture sawn through the doubled planking, and in the fragments of casks and cases with which the ice was bestrewn around. There was a board, too, with writing upon it, nailed up conspicuously; but I tried in vain to decipher it. Under the impulse of strong excitement, I again turned abruptly toward my guide; this time, I could not obtain a glimpse of him. Methought, however, that I heard a rustle like the sound of wings, and that the inflated silk over my head became suddenly tinted with the hues of the rainbow. And so I knew that I was under the guidance of Hope; and that Despair would trouble me no more. Whither my countrymen were gone I could not conjecture; but, at least, I deemed them safe.

———————————

Away, and away, we soared upwards and sped onwards; how far, and how long, I marked not. And lo, another object! not a ship—it is a house, this time; yes, a house in the lonely wilderness of that frozen ocean, a hut upon the waves of that boundless *mer de glace*. And it was fashioned in rude form; and the material was rough blocks of ice; and snow seemed to have been used as their cement. The roof was formed by poles and spars; and across them yet hung a sailcloth covering. Roundabout the hut was a lofty wall, built apparently to shelter it from storms, and snowdrifts; and the wall was built with the same material as the house, for Nature's plentiful quarry fails not in those Polar regions, if man's hand and man's axe be brought there, to hew and shape. But for whom the shelter, and whither had they gone, who tenanted it? I knew well that the long lost had been here. None but they—no miserable, wandering tribe of Esquimaux—could have left such unmistakable marks of forethought, and skill, and energy. Near by, too, was plainly visible the icy cradle wherein a vessel had been lying, and on an even keel. But ships and men were gone— gone, but how gone, and whither? Earnestly did I gaze for some solution of this mystery; and at length I solved it, ay, plain enough; a line along the surface of the ice became distinctly visible, rugged and indented indeed, but straight, and stretching far away to the Westward. Then was I assured that Sir John and his brave comrades had been here, that they had cut out a channel for their barque, and that the ice had closed in behind them, so soon as they had passed on their way. Yes, I was on their track. And again I heard the soft rustling of the wings of Hope; and the rainbow-tinted hues of the balloon were three-fold more brilliant than before.

One other circumstance only could I note, ere we sped away again upon the search—all who came hither had not departed hence. Side by side, in a sheltered nook, beneath a towering pinnacle of ice, two wooden crosses, peering above the snow, told plainly that beneath it two of the Mariners were sleeping in death. And their names were rudely carved upon the crosses; but again my sight, though in some respects preternaturally sharpened, refused to satisfy my curiosity. Never mind, thought I, 'tis a small proportion in so large a company. We must all die once; and those who rest here, rest as well as though they were laid beneath the "long-drawn aisle;" and their bodies are more enduringly embalmed by the servants of the great Frost-King, than in olden days they could have been by the hand of the cunning men of Egypt.

―――――――――――――

Upwards, and onwards, and steering ever a Westwardly course. And lo, at length—oh, God be praised—yes I found the men I sought! Yes—no more doubt—there I saw them below me, although, with the caprice incident to dreams, I was prevented from dropping down in the midst of them, or rendering myself either visible or audible.

A strange scene it was, independent of its surpassing interest. Rocky islands—vast packs and floes of ice—a lone ship beset, impeded, entangled—a hundred pairs of lusty arms at work with ice-saws and axes, striving to extricate her, by cutting a channel in the direction where open water was visible. A little apart from the busy groups stood one whom I instantly recognised as the Chief. Care had furrowed his brow, and somewhat whitened his locks, and bowed his vigorous form; but manly resolution was stamped upon his features, and command was in every gesture. Bethink you how I strove to shout—how I struggled even to throw myself down into their arms; but the dream-spell was on me; I was invisible, perforce, and my tongue refused to give utterance.

How I watched them! and look, the burly seaman who is a few steps ahead of his comrades, tracking out the pathway to be dug—look, he starts as though a rattlesnake were issuing from the snow under his feet. What is it? He stoops, and I see his big brown hand tremble, as it assuredly would not have done, if picking up a burning grenade. What is it, bold tar, that moves thee thus? Ay, I see now, and know the cause, 'tis yonder little slip of gay coloured silk on which are printed a few short words. Jack could not read, it was evident enough; but he held up his prize, and called out something which I could not hear, and his mess-mates bounded to the spot. Foremost in the race was an athletic young man, in the threadbare uniform of a Midshipman, who had left his father's halls, five years ago, a beardless boy. Nor was the Chieftain himself the last. How did it pass rapidly from hand to hand, that little silken slip! How did its fall amongst them seem to change the whole spirit of the scene! But look again, a gesture from the Chief, not as one of authority this time, but rather as one of suggestion. It is obeyed, however, and a hundred heads are bared; and by the movements of their lips, I could see that every living man amongst them ejaculated a hearty "amen" to the Chieftain's short but earnest thanksgiving to Heaven, for the assistance now known to be at hand. Then I remembered that the brave Sir John was a pious and a God-fearing man; and that the veriest infidel sneers not at religion in the mouth of him, whose heart is fearless and true.

Visible to me, if not audible, what extravagant demonstrations of joy ensued! I felt my little car vibrating to their force, as cheers, peal upon peal, came rolling up into the welkin. Singular was it, too, that though in my dream my ears were stopped, I could read in the expressive features of those rejoicing Mariners their varied emotions, as they vociferated their glee. I could see in their honest countenances, which cheer was for Old England—which for their Queen—which for their homes—which for their wives and little ones. Then they burst forth into grotesque dancing, and slapping of each others' hands, and jumping on to each others' backs, and a thousand merry antics, as though they were children just let loose from school. And anon, in their mirth, running races hither and thither, one, an officer amongst them, picked up another printed silken slip, in general aspect like the former, but addressed, it seemed, to the Chieftain by name. A second look would have been sufficient to master its contents, but the young man looked not the second time, he hurried with it straightway to Sir John. Rare instance this, methought, of the working of a high sense of honour!

And the veteran, what did it convey to him? I saw not; but I saw a tear course down his furrowed cheek; and for the moment my ears were opened to hear his half-smothered ejaculation, "Jane, Jane, God bless thee—true wife, noble woman—we shall meet, thank God, we shall meet!"

So I watched the merry throng, and strove in vain to catch portions of their earnest talk. Suddenly, all eyes were turned upon the Captain; he was speaking, and pointing to the West. A few words only seemed to come from his lips; but those surely were words of command. In a moment, every man, though half delirious with delight, seized upon his axe or his saw. Work recommenced; labour was distributed in gangs. Every arm was vigorously plied. The watch, descended from the mast-head to hear the wondrous tidings, mounted lustily again to his look-out station. Each man was busy at his post; and though there was perchance some display of increased energy and activity, you would not have surmised that these patient labourers had just exchanged the gathering gloom of Despair for the radiant smiles of Hope. O gallant hearts of oak, thought I—resolute, unflinching, enduring, in the prospect of the dreariest of fates—orderly, obedient, loyal, in the thrill of unexpected deliverance.

The remainder of my dream came upon me in snatches.

Midway in a narrow strait, between lofty and sterile banks, a battered and crippled barque was steering South. I knew the place to be Behring's Straits, the vessel the Discovery Ship that I had just left amidst the ice. So bruised, however, was she, so rent, and strained, and maltreated, that but for the friendly aid of a consort's tow-rope, she could scarcely have adventured even on this comparatively easy navigation. At her peak floated the standard of England; but I strove in vain to make out the colours of her welcome escort. Once, I thought I saw plainly the Stars and Stripes of America; but these either faded away, or assumed the appearance of the double-headed eagle of Russia. Be that as it may, my sense of hearing was restored; and I could both hear and see signs of continuous rejoicing and festivity. Sounds of mirth, and song, and music, came upwards to me from those pleasant waters. Many a canoe, too, filled with outlandish people, visited the ships; all was wonder, and delight, and congratulation.

———————————

Hitherto there had been some consistency in my dream; for if my mode of seeing were dream-like and fantastical, what I saw had the verisimilitude of reality. But this was over, or at least was changed. In place of being seated in the car of a balloon, I was now in the maintop of Sir John's battered and leaky ship, a witness to what could only have existence in the wild imaginings of a vision. For, methought we were still steering to the South, when on our larboard hand uprose a range of lofty hills, upon which it seemed to me that I could almost have jumped. Down their sides rolled hundreds of little streams; and in the waters, waist-deep, were myriads of human beings, delving, and scraping, and washing, and picking up what seemed to me to be gold. But they paused in their busy occupations, when they saw the approach of the ships; and, holding up shining masses of the golden ore, shouted to the long missing mariners to come to the mines, and gather a plentiful harvest after their toils. Yardarm were we to the glittering hill-sides, and the miners wore the air of men who rarely tempted in vain; but the crew of the worn-out ship gaily shook their heads, laughed a pleasant little laugh of defiance, and the words, "home, home," came floating up to me from her deck.

———————————

Another trial. The men had theirs, and were staunch. It was the master's turn. Heading still to the southwards, but almost becalmed, I saw a swift steamer ranging fast up with us from astern. This time the Stars and Stripes were plainly evident. She came alongside. Her captain was on our deck in a moment, and engaged in earnest conversation with the good Sir John. By the wave of his hand and a word caught here and there, I knew that the kindly American was pressing the veteran to take passage in his steamer. He drew a little almanac from his pocket, and there seemed to be some comparison as to dates; but Sir John finally, with a moistened eye, touched the other on the shoulder, pointed upwards to the British ensign, and firmly shook his head. Away rushed the friendly steamer, and the crowding passengers on her deck took leave of us with reiterated cheers.

———————————

My dream was drawing to a close; but I yet was housed snugly in my new position, when the look-out at the mast-head announced a sail. It might have been the same day, or the next, or a week later. But he announced a sail—then another—and another—and lastly a steamer under canvas. The squadron bore down upon us. It consisted of two line-of-battle-ships, a frigate, and a screw-propeller, under command of the British Admiral in the Pacific. The greetings and salutes were over, and official etiquette was somewhat relaxed under the intense excitement of the moment, when I heard in my dream, on the quarter-deck of the flag ship, the Admiral thus addressed the carpenter, with a certain meaning twinkle in his eye. "That leaky old tub can never swim round Cape Horn, Carpenter." "I think not, your Honour," discreetly replied Mr. Chips. "Youngster," continued the Admiral turning quickly to a little middy, "go to Captain B. with my compliments, and tell him to call an immediate survey on the Discovery Ship." The little middy touched his cap respectfully, and off he jumped with his message. "Mr. C.," cried the Admiral to the other midshipman who stood by the signal-locker, "signalize the propeller to light her fires, and get up all steam." In thirty seconds four bits of bunting flew out from the mizen royal-mast head.

———————————————

The last object that I saw in my vision was the figure of a woman, walking the ramparts of an old Spanish city on the Pacific coast of Central America. Matronly, and dignified in her air and bearing, her featured bore the impress of past anxiety, but across them flitted at times the consciousness of approaching joy. She gazed wistfully ever and anon seaward; and my heart yearned to tell her all that I had so lately seen. The herd of vulgar gold- hunters, who thronged the battlements, respected her, for her long-continued sorrows, her abiding faith, her matchless perseverance. They pressed not on her steps.

I, too, who knew more than they did, how I longed to see the meeting—but no, no, 'twere better that it should be sacred.

I had not the choice; at this moment, forced upon my unwilling ears, through the key-hole came a tiny voice, "Please, Sir, mother says won't you get up; the stage will be here in ten minutes."

———————————————

WOMAN NEVER AT A LOSS.

An Eastern Apologue—From the French.

—-I read her my manuscript; I had been abusing woman I must confess. Not a single good word could I say for the sex; and long did my companion and I battle the point. Many truisms, much that was strictly veritable had I brought forward, and she had been obliged to yield to the justice of almost all my remarks, though disclaiming against my slander at the same time. Finally —"You intend to marry, yourself?" she asked.

"Certainly," I replied; "to find a woman bold enough to take me, after having convinced her that I knew all the duplicity of the sex, will henceforward be the dearest of my hopes."

"Is this resignation or fatuity?"

"That is my secret."

"Well, then," she said, "most learned doctor of conjugal arts and sciences, permit me to relate to you a little Eastern apologue, that I read long ago in a small volume that was offered to us every year in the shape of an almanac." I bowed my delighted attention. The pretty creature threw herself back in her *chaise longue*, rested her little feet upon the fender, and fixed her arch dark eyes upon me.

"At the commencement of the Empire," she began, "the ladies brought into fashion a game which consisted in accepting nothing from the person with whom one agreed to play, without saying the word 'Iadeste.' An affair of this kind lasted, as you may suppose, whole weeks, and the height of cleverness was to surprise one another into receiving a trifle without uttering the magic word."

"Even a kiss?"

"Oh! I have twenty times gained 'Iadeste' in that way," said she, laughing. "It was, I believe, about this time, apropos of this game of which the origin is either Arabian or Chinese, that my apologue obtained the honours of print."

"But if I tell it to you," she interrupted, looking doubtfully at me, and passing her taper finger slowly across her lips, with a charmingly coquettish gesture, "promise me to insert it at the end of your book!"

"Will you not be bestowing a treasure? I owe you already so many obligations, I do not hesitate to add this; therefore, I accept it at once." She smiled maliciously, and went on in these words.

"A philosopher had compiled a very large collection of all the tricks our sex can play; and so, to guard himself against our wiles, he carried this constantly about him. One day, in travelling, he found himself near an Arabian encampment. A young woman, sitting under the shade of a palm-tree, got up suddenly, on the approach of the stranger, and invited him so obligingly to repose under her tent that he could not resist accepting. The husband of this lady was then absent. The philosopher had scarcely established himself upon the soft carpets, when his graceful hostess presented him with fresh dates and a vessel full of milk; he could not help seeing the rare perfection of the hands which offered the beverage and the fruit. But to recover from the confusion into which the charms of the young Arabian had thrown him, and whose snares he began to dread, the wise man drew out his book and read! The enchanting creature, piqued at this disdain, said to him in the sweetest voice, 'That book must be very interesting, since it seems to be the only thing you consider worthy of notice. Would it be an indiscretion to ask the name of the science of which it treats!' The philosopher replied without raising his eyes, 'The subject of this book is beyond the comprehension of woman.' This refusal excited more and more the curiosity of the young Arabian. She put forward the prettiest little foot that ever left its transient trace upon the fleeting sands of the desert. The sage began to waver; his truant looks would wander toward those dainty feet till his eyes, too powerfully tempted, finally mingled the flame of their admiration with the fire that darted from the ardent and black orbs of the young Asiatic. Again, then, she asked in her soft low tones, 'what is the book?' and the charmed philosopher replied, 'I am the author of this work. It contains a record of all the tricks that woman ever invented!'

"'What! all—absolutely all?' inquired the daughter of the desert.

"'Yes—all! And it is only in studying woman constantly, that I have been able to overcome my fear of them.'

"'Ah!' said the Arabian, dropping the long lashes of her snowy eyelids; and then throwing suddenly upon the pretended sage the full lustre of her Eastern eyes she made him forget in one instant his valuable book and its invaluable contents. Behold my philosopher the most impassioned of men!

"Thinking that he perceived in the manner of his young hostess a slight touch of coquetry, the stranger hazarded an avowal of his adoration. How could he have resisted? The sky was so blue, the sand shone in the distance like a blade of gold; the wind brought love upon its wings, and the wife of the absent Arab seemed to reflect all the brilliancy with which she was surrounded. Her bright eyes, too, became liquid; and she seemed, by a slight movement of her graceful head, to consent to listen to the honeyed words of the quondam philosopher.

"The wise man was in a full tide of eloquence when the distant gallop of a horse was heard rapidly approaching.

"'We are lost!' cried the alarmed Fatima; 'my husband is coming. He is jealous as a tiger, and still more fierce. In the name of the Prophet, and if you love your life, hide yourself in this chest!' The frightened author, seeing nothing else to do, rushed into the chest; his hostess shut it down, locked it, and took the key. She went to meet her spouse, and after several caresses, which put him into the best of humour, 'I must tell you,' said she, 'a very singular adventure.'

"'I listen, my gazelle,' said the Arabian, seating himself upon a cushion and crossing big legs after the Oriental fashion.

"'There came here to-day a kind of philosopher; he pretended to have collected in a book all the treacheries of which my sex is capable; and this false sage—spoke—to—me of love!'

"'Well?'

"'I listened to him!' At these words the Arab bounded like a lion, and drew his kangiar. The philosopher, from the bottom of the chest, heard all, and sent to the devil his book, woman, and all the men of Arabia Petrea.

"'Fatima!' cried the husband, if you wish to live, answer! 'Where is the traitor?'

"Horrified at the storm she had raised, Fatima threw herself at the feet of her lord, and trembling under the menacing steel of the poniard, she pointed out the coffer, with a single look, as prompt as it was timid. Then rising, ashamed, she drew the key from her girdle and gave it to her jealous lord. But—as he turned furiously from her, the malicious beauty burst into a shout of laughter, and laying her white hand upon his shoulder, 'Iadeste!' she exclaimed; 'at last, I shall have my beautiful gold chain! Give it to me; you have lost. Another time, Fazom, have a little better memory!' The husband stupefied, let fall the key, and presenting the golden chain, on his knees, offered his dear Fatima to bring her all the jewels of all the caravans that passed that year, if she would only give up such cruel methods of gaining the 'Iadeste.' Then, as he was an Arabian and did not like to lose his gold chain, though it was to his wife, he remounted his steed and went off, grumbling at his ease in the desert
—for he loved Fatima too much to show her his regrets.

"At last, the young woman released the philosopher more dead than alive from his prison, and said to him, gravely,

"'Mr. Philosopher, don't forgot to insert this trick in your collection.'"

MANDRAGORA—BY THE DOZEN.

And so you cannot coax yourself off to sleep? Why? Were you beguiled by their exquisite flavour into rashly smoking three or four of those potent Regalias, with which your friend, the rich stock-broker, professes to aid the digestion of his guests, after a lengthened sitting at his luxurious table? Or did the rounded arm and taper fingers of his fair wife, presiding over the mysteries of the silver urn, tempt you to indulgence in too frequent cups of Souchong? Perhaps you are endeavouring, in spite of yourself, to solve some knotty problem in politics, or love, or chess, or mathematics. Perhaps you have a considerable bill to take up to-morrow, with a very slim balance at your banker's. Perhaps you have a heart-ache; perhaps a head-ache. At any rate, your nerves and senses are painfully strained; and you feel as though you would give the world and all, for a lullaby that would serve its purpose. My good Sir, compose your mind. If you can't sleep and dream, as you desire— dream and sleep. Reverse, I say, the common order. And do not sneer at the suggestion, unless you prefer tossing about all night in vain. The process is not only not impossible; it is not half so difficult as you might suppose, presuming—as I have a right to presume, in regard to my reader—that your imagination is not hopelessly inert.

Some persons recommend to the restless and wide-awake the repetition of scraps from books, in prose or verse, just as though every one had a plenteous store of "elegant extracts" garnered up in his memory, and as though authors specially aimed at being somniferous. There are indeed not a few among them, who unavoidably achieve this distinction; and the advice might not really be bad, if you could con over—once would be sufficient—Mr. A.'s last pamphlet on political economy, or the Rev. Mr. B.'s last sermon. On the whole however, inasmuch as your favourite passages—should you know any of them by heart—may be the very opposite of soothing in their tendencies, this mode of wooing slumber can scarcely be pronounced successful.

You must commence, I say, by dreaming, if you would compel yourself gently to sleep; but before I proceed to introduce to you my list of available prescriptions in this line, I note one with which my readers may possibly be familiar, having learned it in their school-boy days. You will not now be told for the first time, that a drowsy sensation may be induced by musing upon— or dreaming of, which is the same thing—a field of tall and ripe barley, swept by fresh autumnal gales. The rise and fall of each bowed head, with its feathery and graceful spikes, combines well with the undulating motion of the whole and the varied play of light and shade. The idea is otherwise expressed by the British Laureate in "The Poet's Song," one of his minor pieces; "and waves of shadow," says he, "went over the wheat." Nevertheless it is clear that he missed the proper application of the thought, for, in place of lulling the beholder to forgetful repose, the sight seems to have made him break out into a song so loud that wild swans paused to listen in their flight, larks fluttered down to earth, swallows gave up hunting bees, snakes slipped under sprays, wild hawks stared over sparrows stricken under their claws, and the very nightingales were set a-thinking. Truly a sad perversion this of a golden opportunity! But your rhymsters were ever a crazy race. When they deal with their fellows generally, we all know how they botch poor human nature. What, then, can be expected, when poets undertake to figure out one of themselves? Still, let us improve the occasion. Barley-fields or wheat-fields are well enough in their way; only, if you conjure up this image, I would advise you to season it with an abundance of red poppies intermingled with the legitimate crop, and a very careful attempt on your part to number these interlopers one by one, preparatory, if so it please you, to flipping off their heads. With due allowance, therefore, for its lack of novelty, this dream may be admitted into our collection.

And it may be proper to remark at the outset that, though the dreams whereof I propose to treat are sufficiently distinct in their kind, it is desirable, in the practical use of them, to run them one into another—to fuse them unconsciously as it were, without being over-nice as to the point at which one ends and another begins. It is not requisite, however, for this reason, that they should all be packed into one paragraph, like a daily paper's report of one of Mr. Morrill's speeches on the Tariff, or a Secretary of the Treasury's Report. You shall have each dainty conceit served up in its own dish, so that, furthermore by the way, you can take them in such order as suits your own good pleasure. This view of the matter relieves me also from the necessity of formal arrangement. It is altogether unimportant which fancy comes uppermost. The main thing is to shut off all thought concerning the actualities of life, eschewing reference to your loves, your hates, your wrestlings with circumstance, your mental cares, your bodily ailments. I repeat it: you must dream, if you would sleep. Counting the breezy barley-field above mentioned as one, I believe I can supply you with a dozen subjects.

Your physical eye is closed, of course—your mind's eye being, on that account, all the more keenly alive to impression, and the better able to compass an unembarrassed range. Set it, then, upon a spiral stairway endless so far as I can imagine it, though you may perchance by looking earnestly upward discover whereto it leads, or by peering intently downward find out its base. But did I say a stairway? That was not what I meant; and dreamers, of all men, are at liberty to change or modify their views. I should have said an inclined plane. Let it be steep, smooth, slippery, broad enough to admit the passage of several figures simultaneously, and guarded by bannisters on either side. When, fatigued with the vain attempt to satisfy your doubts as to the safety of this strange structure, your curiosity craves enlightenment as to its uses, I pray you to observe how I would have it peopled. Sliding tumultuously adown the balustrades, lo and behold an innumerable throng of Cherubs in unbroken succession, coming whence and going whither you know not, but each the counterpart of his predecessors, and each flapping his little wings to maintain his balance, rendered precarious as it is by his inability to sit a-straddle. As for the inclined plane itself thus fantastically flanked, you soon perceive that it is the *via sacra* of many an Ethardo, whom you have known in the flesh or in the spirit—Ethardo, the marvellous gymnast, who mounted and descended steep slopes at the Sydenham Crystal Palace, by trundling inflated balls beneath his feet. Up and down, down and up, some painfully and some skilfully pediculating, your Ethardi pass and repass each other, disorderly yet in order. Name them and salute them as they go by. You have probably more acquaintances among them than I; but I recognise Robinson Crusoe and Count Bismarck, Tarquinius Priscus and Horace Greeley, John Ruskin and Lucrezia Borgia, Mrs. Fry and Edgar Poe, Mr. Gladstone and Dion Boucicault, John Bright and Mrs. Grundy, Ben. Wade and Victor Hugo, Pio Nono and the Great Mogul. Note, too, the various material moulded into circular form, and blown up by way of ambulant footstool; now it is a crown, now a crozier, now a bag of gold, now a wind-bag, now a woman's heart, now a man's fame done up in a newspaper and properly puffed. Ring the changes upon these Ethardi and the motive power that each applies, O my wakeful friend; and at least you may lose sight of your own individuality. Or, take a slide down the banisters with the young Cherubs, and perchance you may touch bottom—in Lethe.

Not so? Let us proceed. There's a man at our Club, whose reputation is so solidly built up, though on an ethereal basis, that I never knew any one presume to question it. He is an absolute master of one accomplishment; unrivalled, and—to the best of my belief, though I can't vouch for the fact— unenvied. Admiring spectators gather round him and applaud; but, if he have ambitious imitators, they rehearse in secret. So far, he does well—ay, with consummate tact and unfailing certainty—what few men can do at all, unless once in a while at dreary intervals, and then by accident. Not to keep you in suspense, which is antagonistic to repose and slumber, this young paragon contrives to throw off his cigar-smoke from his lips, at will, in an unerring series of the most lovely rings or wreaths, which, as they float and rise in tremulous succession, strangely fascinate the looker-on. It may be that this feat is not much of an achievement, morally or physically or intellectually considered. It may be also that the Club does not do itself much honour, in setting so high a value on this performance. But what will you? In the palmy days of Greece, a man acquired a certain celebrity by his precision and address in throwing peas through a needle's eye—the peas being, I presume, much smaller or the needles much larger, than any with which we sow or make soup in these degenerate days. Still, so highly do I appreciate perseverance in the acquirement of any difficult art, that I purpose doing much more for my proficient in smoke, than was done for his man of peas by Philip of Macedon. That bushel of ammunition was a scurvy reward. I confer immortality, by thus registering a fact and hinting a name. And I do this from a sense of gratitude, wherein I trust that you will participate, so soon as you perceive the connection that may surely be traced, between the smoke thus artistically and gracefully jetted into air, and the drowsiness by which you would fain be possessed. Do but imagine a score of your acquaintances round a table, each an adept in this way, and each filling the atmosphere with coronet after coronet of vapour thrown up from meerschaum or cheroot. Whose are the most frequent, whose the most perfect, whose retain their form the longest? Watch the little circlets as they wave and tremble; and award the palm of merit fairly. Nay, even if you tell me that you are innocent of the weed and nauseated by its odour, none the less shall this fantasy be available. I saw once a ship-of-war firing a salute; and lo, from one of the guns went up to the pure sky, in magnified proportions, just such a wreath as those I have described, as delicate yet as clearly defined, and touched withal with a suspicion of prismatic colours as it caught the rays of the sun. An enthusiastic painter might have deemed it an invisible Fairy's aureole; a sentimental milliner would have set it down as the flounce of her unseen robe. Whether the gunner of this occasion had taken a lesson from my friend at the Club, I cannot pretend to decide; I only assure you that I witnessed the phenomenon. You have, therefore, but to multiply as well as magnify. Think of a squadron, a fleet, all the navies of the world, sailing slowly and majestically in unending circuit, as the custom is when they bombard some hapless fort. The saluting is continuous; the movement never ceases; but the big cannon are noiseless now and harmless. Space is joyous with the innumerable wreaths of bluish vapour; but the red slaughter and the accursed tumult of the sea-fight are not heard or seen. Ponder long and lazily, I counsel you, over the evolutions of the ships and the convolutions of the smoke. Those may lure you, possibly, into the Waters of Oblivion; these may spirit you away to the land of the Lotos-Eaters.

Another dream invites you; but it must be sketched with more reticence, and this for two reasons. In the first place, the subject has become identified with that portion of theatrical entertainments usually found to be the least soporific. In the second place, if your imagination were encouraged to free range hereupon, you might be foolish enough to connect its poetic motion and its charm with certain souvenirs of a certain fair friend of yours, whom it were wiser to forget if you desire to profit by this Mandragorean system. Briefly, then, I commend a Ballet, as not altogether unworthy of trial—but not, be it observed, that thing of gas lamps, and pink tights, and leers, and *poses plastiques*, over which young America goes into raptures. By no means. Picture to yourself a smooth sward beneath clustered pines, a tender moonlight, and Nymphs—not semi-nude as is the fashion of our day, neither affecting the contortions of the gymnast as in our modern caricature of dancing—but robed in swansdown, with nodding plumes and tasseled fuschias pendent, tripping it, if you will, on "light fantastic toe," yet through stately and solemn measures. You remember Giulio Romano's dance of Apollo and the Muses in the Pitti at Florence? Take that for your model; then place the figures to your liking. Nor forget to add an orchestra of Æolian harps. Let them hang among the pine-branches, and sigh forth Weber's Last Waltz, just to set the groups in motion. Then fail not in your breathings, O soft night-wind; foot it daintily, ye wildwood Nymphs—so may sleep steal gently upon the restless one, while yet his ear and eye are unsated!

Another dream: blue water again, though, this time, with a golden beach. It is calm; but the surf rolls in languidly, with low murmurous sound, as it will roll, be the sea's surface never so smooth, beyond the involuntary breakers. What graceful bends and curves are marked, for an instant, with frothy pencil, upon the shining sands! How they sparkle with evanescent light! How soon the tiny bubbles disappear! But you have watched all this, many and many a time; and stale indeed hereon were description and moralizing! Why, then, this present allusion? What is there in it, tending to lull the acuter sensibilities? What offers it of gently-soothing exercise to the overwrought and throbbing brain? This is the reply. Popular belief gives to every ninth or tenth wave, tumbling in upon the shore, supremacy over its fellows. It swells up into fuller volume. It sweeps landward with a more majestic force. This is the story; but I would have you test its correctness. Is it the ninth, or the tenth? So, lie down yonder upon the mass of dry sea-weed piled against the rocks, and count patiently a dozen, a score, a hundred, a thousand waves as they come in. You shall tell me, to-morrow morning, whether the ninth have it, or the tenth—whether there be any regularity at all.

Again: if we do not, like the Roman Augurs, watch and interpret the flight of birds as of good or evil omen, some of them—I mean some of the birds, not of the Augurs—may help us to become, for a while, independent of fate and fortune. Did you ever, for instance, sit at a window on a summer's evening, and take note how a flight of swallows skims the air? They are not very numerous, perhaps; but as they dart to and fro, and cross and recross before you, their number appears indefinite, and the zigzag peculiarity of their movements can only be verified by the closest possible scrutiny. I have satisfied myself that the motion is regular, and that it describes an elongated figure of 8, traced as I am sure you have often traced it upon ice with the outer edge of your skates. Now, though I tell you this on the faith of my own personal observation, you are not bound to accept my word for it. Dream therefore that, while you are blending two ovals into one figure upon the frozen pond, swallows overhead are keeping time to your gyrations. The winter sport and the summer bird may be made to harmonize, as it is only in a dream; and close watching will enable you hereafter to support or disavow my theory.

Again: return, if you please, from air to water, for you have by no means exhausted the resources of this latter element, in the way of material for dreams. Are you an angler? Did you never drowse and doze over your rod, when "sitting in a pleasant shade," on a sultry afternoon, not a nibble disturbed the equanimity of your float? The mere thought were suggestive of a nap—suggestive, that is, to the indolently disposed, with whom however you may not be classed, seeing that your mind is in a state of unwholesome excitement, the which it is my business to allay. And so, I pray you, look deeper into this matter; pry down into the blue transparent depths, and mark the fish that swarm about your hook. Is it paste thereon, or a wriggling worm? Never mind; the bait is singularly attractive. To say nothing of the float gently bobbing ever and anon, and of the tell-tale ripples rising to the surface, you can see with your own eyes how victims dally with temptation; how they course to and fro, and round and round; how one eyes the bait, and another smells it, and another mumbles it; how one swims away, and presently returns, and with him his mate in size and colour. Are they over-fed or over- cautious, that they thus play round, but will not gorge? Does one egg on his brother to try the suspicious morsel, hoping himself to profit by his brother's experience? Is there so much resemblance to human foibles discernible down there, among these poor little inhabitants of the waters under the Earth? The question is worth studying out—especially by a sleepless man, who, while contemplating the forms, the motions, the manners, and the minds of fish, may unconsciously swallow the bait that is thus dropped before him.

It was my intention to devote a long and distinct paragraph to each of four other subjects, that appear to me no less adapted for the consideration of waking dreamers. These are, respectively, Ghosts, Labyrinths, Regattas, and the Eleven Thousand Virgins of Cologne. But it is well to leave something to the reader's perspicacity and inventive powers. Indeed, why should he not fancy—dream is the more appropriate term—that he himself has undertaken to complete these special paragraphs? Let his imaginary pen glide, swift and effortless, over his imaginary foolscap. Ten to one, he will fill in and elaborate my outlines, far better than I could work them out myself. For instance, I do but mention Ghosts; he might summon to his presence, and bid troop before him, hosts upon hosts of his friends or relatives, or of his chosen heroes and heroines in romance and history. He might clothe them in white or in grey; he might attire them in their ordinary habiliments; in short, he might parade them according to his own taste, without reference to mine, which whould be a clear point in his favour. Accidentally, I might call up some spirit that had vexed and thwarted him through life, for no man whose experience is worth remembering hath not had his enemies, hidden or revealed, and very few are the men, fewer the women, who have never disposed of a rival. My reader of the moment, invested with my functions, will of course evoke none but his familiars, the well-bred and well-behaved. Let me be grateful accordingly that, by transferring the responsibility to him, I escape the chance of bringing forward, innocently and inopportunely, some social Banquo. And so I pass on, with one single word of caution to my substitute in completing this paragraph: let him not convert his pen into a Pre-Raphaelitish paint-brush. Airy beings must be rather hinted than described. The realism of anatomical plates, applied to them, would spoil the reader's dream *in toto*, and wake him up perhaps more hopelessly than ever.—As to Labyrinths, the course is obvious. Take a dozen of these quaint contrivances, and place them side by side, as Paulsen or Paul Morphy may place the sundry chess-boards whereat he is to play, simultaneously and blindfolded, an equivalent number of games. Pop, over the hedges and into the very core of each one, any personage against whom you have a grudge, or any one of the Ghosts just convened that may have been troublesome; and then challenge the incarcerated individuals to find their way out of limbo, by the gravelled pathways. Should one of the whole number emerge, through extraordinary good luck, quietly tip him back again over the hedge, or defy him to retrace his steps and regain the centre. You may enlarge this suggestion, I think, into a paragraph reasonably long.— The same with Regattas. I am almost sorry that I gave up to you so felicitous a topic; for all ages and all waters may be laid under contribution. From Noah's Ark shall float the commodore's broad pendant. The ocean shall be covered, so far as eye can range, with countless craft of every build and rig. And all shall glide about in quiet, inasmuch as oars shall be muffled, and steamers, having learned to consume their own smoke, shall be taught equally to swallow their hideous noises. The marshalling of the competitors and the order of the racing are left to your discretion; but there need be no lack of interest. Caiques from Stamboul and gondolas from Venice shall be frequent; and pirogues from the Malayan peninsula shall over-haul the three trim yacht- schooners that raced across the Atlantic from New-York. Here Cleopatra's barge shall be matched against an Esquimaux kayak; there a catamaran from

Coringa shall bump the Yale College eight. If you cannot make something out of all this picturesque confusion, and if you cannot contrive to lose therein both yourself and the reader of your paragraph, the fault will be yours, not mine.— There remain the Eleven Thousand Virgins of Cologne. What are you to do with them? Simply this. Endow each one of them with personal attributes; let each have form and features, distinct from the others of her sisterhood. Is the task difficult? So much the better. After a cool thousand or so of these individual portraitures, you may begin to fumble in vain for separate identities. In fact, who knows whether you may not be compelled to take refuge hopelessly in sleep, the very mark at which both cf us are aiming?

And now, the foregoing long and subdivided paragraph being brought at last to an end, it were disingenuous to shirk an admission, that the "who's who" is not so plainly discernible therein as it might be. You and I, and the reader and the writer, and the giver and recipient of advice, will be accused by the critic of being somewhat queerly mixed up. What, then? Are not vagueness and uncertainty of style specially appropriate to the circumstances? Who would thank us for precision? No, no; carry clearness, if you like, into your mathematical definitions; but leave us our mistiness when we treat of the mysterious. Nor, on the whole, am I otherwise than content with my suggested assumption of temporary and imaginary authorship, as one of the methods for quieting a fevered brain. How pleasant to dream that rival Publishers are contending for your manuscript poems; that rival Managers are waylaying you for a sight of your unwritten comedy! Besides, by adding authorship to the list that closed with the damsels of Cologne, the number is brought up to eleven, so that, when I wind up with my trump card, the promised dozen of dreams will be complete, and I shall be enabled to dispense with the "waves of shadow" on the wheat-field, which I acknowledged were not my original conception.

But am I too late in bringing forward my last and happiest idea?—though for that matter, when the tale of Mazeppa was concluded, "the King had been an hour asleep," and yet Mazeppa's story was told out ne'ertheless. For your immediate purpose therefore, or for use on your next sleepless night, I entrust you with the crowning opiate. Recollect that you are dreaming; and dream that all your intimates and relatives, all of whom you have ever heard or read with interest, men and women and children, people of every age and clime— imagine them, I say, all seated before you at a round table. How any table is to accommodate so vast a multitude, is their affair, and yours; the dreamer is never baulked by technical impediments. Have your eye upon them all at once —another little difficulty, to be overcome only by mortals in the incipient stage of somnolency. Or, if your mind's eye obstinately refuses to enlarge its orbit in this direction, so as to embrace such a vast and heterogeneous assemblage, gather, I beseech you, into one focus any such crowd as you habitually see. The Sunday audience of the Reverend Henry Ward Beecher will answer the purpose; or you may fancy yourself at one of the old Tammany Hall Meetings; or at the Opera, on a fashionable night; or in the Senate at Washington during the impeachment of Mr. Johnson. It matters not when and where; but the proceedings strike you as insufferably dull, and you give vent to your feelings in a yawn that may neither be suppressed nor concealed. Suddenly, moved by the same impulse and unable also to control or hide its effect, the jaw of every soul present is dropped to the lowermost, and all mouths are open in a universal yawn. It is not catching; it is caught. Beecher gapes, and the elect are gaping round him. Isaiah Rynders the same, and the same with his "unterrified" hearers. Parepa-Rosa stands open- mouthed in dumb show of singing, while humming-birds perched on chignons vibrate, as they vainly try to resist the irresistible. Gape the Republicans, and gape the Democrats, in response to the gaping Butler on his legs. There is, in Shakespeare's words—though his ignorant editors have transformed it into a "gap"—there is, I say, "a gape in Nature." Will you alone hold out: I can't believe it. You have yawned in concert, I am morally certain. Indeed, if, as these long-drawn prescriptions come to an end, you be not far on the road to forgetfulness, I can give you but one parting counsel. Nothing else can serve and save you—you must incontinently take morphine.

DOCTOR PABLO'S PREDICTION.

Doctor Pablo went back a lonely man, to his old mother, in France, after having passed twenty years in the Philippines.—
English magazine.

He did so. We can vouch thus much for the correctness of *Household Words* of the 6th inst., whence the above-named quotation is copied. And as the subject of it is a remarkable personage, and this unexpected meeting with him in print has revived in us not a few pleasant recollections, we will take the liberty of informing our readers how we came to have personal knowledge of Don Pablo—for this, and not Doctor Pablo, was his cognomen, at least amongst his friends.

Embarking at Bombay, many a long year since, in the East India Company's steamer *Atalanta*, for passage up the Red Sea, we soon fell into acquaintance with a party of foreigners, partially isolated as they were from the crowd of Anglo-Indians—men, women, and children—returning by the over-land route to their native country. They (the foreigners) were five in number, two Frenchmen, two Dutchmen, and a Spaniard. Of the three last-mentioned we have small recollection. Of the Frenchmen, one was Don Pablo.

The other, who headed the whole party, was Monsieur Adolphe Barrot, a brother of Odilon and Ferdinand Barrot, whose names are familiar to those conversant with recent French history. He was at the time bound to Paris, on leave, from his post of Consul-General at Manila. At an early period of his career he had been attached to the French Legation at Washington, or at least had travelled through this country. Subsequently, when Consul at Carthagena, he distinguished himself by his resolute and humane interposition on occasion of a certain revolutionary outbreak. After his return from the East, he served as French Minister to Naples and to Lisbon, and now, we believe, holds the same appointment at Brussels. Between this man of cultivated mind, polished manners, and companionable qualities, and Don Pablo, whose exterior smacked but little of intercourse with "the world," there was evidently a bond of no common sort. Blunt, earnest, truthful, with quick perceptions and impulses of the kindest nature, there was something very fresh and irresistibly attractive in the character of Don Pablo. We did not wonder at the intimacy. Opposites are drawn together. In friendly and social intercourse the time sped away.

At that period, the steamers bound from Bombay to Suez touched at Cosseir, a port two days' sail South of Suez, and about 150 miles East of Thebes on the Nile. The object was to land passengers who cared to cross the intervening Desert, as the quickest mode of gaining Upper Egypt. To Cosseir we were ourselves destined; our new friends being on their way direct to France, *viâ* Suez, Cairo, and the Mediterranean, and having made none of the ordinary provision for the less-frequented route. But we plied them strongly with argument and entreaty, to divert them from their intended limited course; not forgetting the threat of ridicule in a Parisian drawing-room, where a man who had missed such a chance would never be able to hold up his head. Finally, they consented. After a voyage of sixteen days, the coaling process at Aden included, three groups of travellers landed at Cosseir. We had dealings with two of them.

For although we had persuaded Mr. Barrot, Don Pablo and their associates, to take our route, we could not precisely undertake to accompany them. We were to travel over the same ground, but not together; for we had engaged, ere we left Bombay, to join fortunes with a small party of veterans and valetudinarians who had made elaborate preparations for the journey, and were not sorry to have the aid of one who did not belong to either class, but who was perhaps for that very reason more competent than they themselves to take charge of their caravan. And then there was a lady, and a lady's maid, and a valet, and the thousand and one encumbrances that are incidental to such appendages. What scenes we had with the camel-drivers! What tons of baggage to be loaded! what irritations! what drollery! what delay! Landing early in the morning, the preparations for a start occupied us till a late hour in the afternoon; nor had we ever a more laboursome time of it. Lightly cumbered, and with only a twentieth part of the fuss, Don Pablo and the others had preceded us; but as the same camping-places in this five days' journey are generally frequented, we hoped to see them from time to time. Fortune kindly ordained that we should join them permanently.

It was on a Saturday afternoon that we started from Cosseir, with a train "too numerous to mention." Night had fallen, ere we pitched our tents—the writer sharing that of Sir C. M. At day-light on the following morning, we strolled off to the French encampment; were again pressed to join its occupants; were again compelled reluctantly to refuse. Away they went. We returned to our own quarters, where to our horror, in place of hearing "boot and saddle" sounded, the edict was issued from my lady's tent, that there was to be no marching that day. Bah! how provoking! we could not ask for an honourable discharge; but how we longed to desert! Matters fell out, however, more pleasantly then we had a right to expect. Breakfast was served, with the elaborateness of a *fête champêtre*, at eleven o'clock; and as the hostess gracefully poured out the coffee, the talk turned upon those who had sped onward. Presently, by a lucky chance, it occured to her, or to the nominal head of the party, that dawdling away a Sunday on a barren speck of Mahommedan sand was not in itself the essential duty of a plain Christian, nor specially agreeable to a man whose thoughts were keenly set upon the marvels of Luxor and Karnac. In short, it was mildly suggested to us that, as the organization and first move of the caravan—the real and only difficulties— were accomplished, there would be nothing ungallant in leaving the party to its more orthodox or more leisurely progress. Our coyness may be imagined; but we consented at length to take this view of the matter, and at noon called up our camels. Soon were our trunks and slender stock of kettles and sauce- pans slung upon one; ourselves astride of a second; and on a third, the Arab driver, with whom there was no communicating but by signs. A twelve hours' ride brought us at midnight to the tent of our friends—they having luckily found one available at Cosseir. We raised the canvas from the pegs, and saluted Don Pablo with a "Here I am!" Many years have elapsed since that night, but we can fancy now that we hear his genial rejoinder, "I knew you'd come!" In less time than it takes to tell it, we had edged in our bedding upon the sand, and were one of the Seven—no, six—Sleepers.

Had not a *Howadji* of this Western hemisphere made the Desert and the Nile so peculiarly his own, that it is presumption for a common pen to follow in his track, we might be tempted still further to ransack our memory for pleasant recollections of Don Pablo. Let it suffice to say, that with these pleasant companions we roughed it across the camel-track, in a style of discomfort and good humour rarely surpassed; explored the wonders of Thebes and the Tombs of the Kings; floated down to Cairo; clambered the Great Pyramid; smoked pipes with Pashas; and finally embarked at Alexandria, on the blue waters of the Mediterranean. The farewell was said at Syra, one of the islands of the Ægean. The "five we supped with yesternight" were bound to Malta and Marseilles—we to Athens and Constantinople. As we shook hands at parting with Don Pablo, he quietly remarked, with that cheerful gravity that so well became him, and in allusion to a young lady who had been our three days' acquaintance on board the steamer—*"Adieu, mon cher; vous épouserez Mademoiselle."*

We never saw Don Pablo, but once afterwards. Several months had elapsed. His prophecy had been fulfilled. The lady in question was on our arm, as in sauntering under the arcades of the Palais Royale in Paris, we met our old associate. There was a hearty greeting; but when we reminded him of his prediction and formally introduced him, we remember that he cut the colloquy abruptly short (as it then seemed to us), and turned away with an expression of face for which we were at a loss to account, being ignorant of all the details of his history. Did the memory of the Peninsula of Iala-Iala, and of the loving wife whom he had buried there, fall too suddenly and too sadly upon his sensitive and affectionate spirit?—We cannot say; but this was the beginning and the ending of our knowledge of Doctor Pablo, until we unexpectedly met him in print.

THE NEW HAMPSHIRE ALPS.

It is not very much of a walk from the Glen House up the Eastern face of Mount Washington—less than three hours at a leisurely pace will accomplish it; and on a fine day it would be next to impossible to lose one's-self, if alone. Half the distance or thereabouts, your track lies through a wood, acceptable enough as offering shelter from a July sun, but curtailing your views annoyingly. However, all things end; and if your range of sight be somewhat "cabined, cribbed, confined," at the start, you have no cause for complaint on that score after once emerging from covert, for the rocks, bleak, bare, and irregular, that are scattered all around, though large enough to compel a careful picking of the way between them by no means limit the vision. But the approach has been a hundred times described, and I will only say of it, at the risk of repetition, that he who comes up from the Glen House, and fails to turn his eye continually over his right shoulder, to dwell lovingly upon the near and noble outlines of Mounts Jefferson, Adams, and Madison, has no appreciation of this sort of scenery.

The morning had been superlatively fine, and troops of mounted dames and damsels and cavaliers made the various pathways lively with their glee. But caprice is the rule of these high regions; and when I was within ten minutes of the summit, clouds of misty vapour came suddenly scudding up, whence I knew not, but shutting out a peep here and a vista there, as they caracolled in fantastic evolutions. Presently, to these kaleidoscopic effects succeeded a slight hailstorm—it was rain visibly beneath us, attended with thunder and lightning—but anon all was comparatively clear again, and from the congregated spectators went up many a genuine burst of enthusiastic admiration, as point after point opened out or was shut in by the scud.

The two rough stone buildings upon the small plateau that crowns the mountain, built for the accommodation of travellers, are called respectively the "Summit" and the "Tip-top" House. Once rivals, they now form a single establishment—one being used as a restaurant, the other as a dormitory. On this particular day, nearly a hundred persons must have refreshed themselves in the former—a dozen or fifteen in the latter; and I must own, it was not without a sense of relief that I saw the last of the descending parties set forth about 2 P. M., being myself of the select few about to take the chance of sunset and sunrise.

For the afternoon, then—for the interval of time was to be occupied—a guide was summoned, to show half-a-dozen of us the wonders of Tuckerman's Ravine, a *cul-de-sac* between two great buttresses of Mount Washington, that

prop it up towards the South and West. The sides of this ravine are very precipitous the head of it being formed of layers of rock, at an angle of about ninety-five degrees, over which a cascade precipitates itself, fed by the springs and melted snows above. In the bed of this hollow, to which the descent is sufficiently sharp to gratify the keenest amateur pedestrian, the accumulated snow of the winter, blown over from the impending heights, lies packed in such enormous masses that it seldom entirely disappears until the latter part of August. At the period of my visit, on Friday, the 29th of July, a huge portion thereof remained, and the famous "Snow-Arch" was not only visible but practicable. This natural curiosity is a cave channelled out from the vast snow bank as a passage for the descending waters, the roof of which, gradually melting away, leaves height and space for walking along this gallery as it were in the very bed of the torrent. You enter perforce, be it observed, where the stream emerges. The length was certainly not less than two hundred feet, the breadth of the tunnel perhaps forty or fifty. Of the thickness of the roof I cannot speak, not having essayed it; but the little knot of adventurers trusted that it would not cave-in whilst they were groping their difficult way, one after the other, wet-footed and in semi-obscurity, up-stream, from end to end of the arched way. The object of the exploration it would be difficult to define. It certainly was not scientific; it offered no rare beauties; it might have been very well imagined, without the trouble and subsequent risk
—but it was an adventure, and it had its charm. Day-light appeared as we neared the waterfall—luckily not very full—which, as I have already said, comes down the head of the ravine and is the origin of the "Arch" itself. What next? The snow had separated bodily from the face of the rocks to the width of two or three feet, as you see ice fields in a thaw detach themselves from the land whereto they have been joined. We could therefore emerge, and clamber up the abrupt face of the rocks, though the first start was not inviting, inasmuch as we had to hoist ourselves up by unequal pressure upon soft snow on one side and hard rock on the other. The alternative was a return. This would have been inglorious; up we went. It was a rough business. The guide had been over the ground once before, this season—so he said, at least—but he "harked back" occasionally, as though not quite certain of his way. It seemed impossible to diverge either to the right or left, and so gain the comparatively easier slope. We were doomed to mount, in the hope of finding successive steps, inasmuch as a retracing of those taken was not for a moment to be thought of; descent in such cases is always far more dangerous and troublesome. It was fortunate that in crossing twice or thrice the waterfall itself, we were not pumped on to any serious extent. I was moistened only, being garnished with a Macintosh; and I have only two scars now left on my shins, the result of scraping too close an acquaintance with sundry rocks. The whole affair lasted between three and four hours. I cannot recommend it, save

to very enthusiastic mountaineers, or to *ci-devant jeunes hommes* anxious to test the effects of Time upon their powers of walking and of endurance.

Regaining the hurricane-deck of the Tip-top House—for the roof is the principal promenade, and often times assuredly deserves the name I give it, how gratefully, as the sun went down, stole the sense of ineffable grandeur over the somewhat wearied frame! It was a superb evening; and though it would not suit me to cull a leaf from the Guide-book, and tell all that is therein narrated, I must mention one particular wherein this locality is notable, if not quite unique. I think I remember something of the kind, but not so marked, at sunrise as seen from the summit of Etna; but not thus, on the Righi and Faulhorn in Switzerland, on the Pic du Midi de Bigorre in the Pyrenees, or on other peaks that I have climbed in the days of long ago, to salute the coming or speed the parting day. The nearest approach to it that I have seen, was at the Great Pyramid of Ghizeh. I allude to the wonderful distinctness and regularity with which the shadow of the great cone itself is traced, at sunset, striding over heights and lowlands, mound and lake—all the intervening surface, in fact, between the spectator and the far distant horizon
—until it contracts almost to a point where earth and sky merge into one. The sharpness of these converging parallel lines of shadow in that luminous atmosphere absolutely astounded me. They were as crisp, as clearly defined, as those that you may see in antique pictures of Jacob's Dream, leading ladder-wise from Heaven to the head of the slumbering Patriarch. Sunrise, next morning—for I was again favoured with clear weather and only sufficient frost to render the roof of the restaurant slightly slippery—sunrise, I say, reserved all this. The narrow lines, now on the Western horizon, broadened out and came upwards and forwards, as in the evening they had elongated and gone down. It was in truth a rare spectacle, not to be forgotten, and individualizes this natural observatory.

As for the view itself, it has been described *ad nauseam*, and I have only a few words to say about it. It happened, as it often does happen, that I fell in with an untravelled admirer of the prospect spread out before us, not charmed however with it more than I was myself. But he would persist in drawing from me an answer to the common question—"how does this compare with some of the famous points of view in the Swiss Alps?" Such tests I hold to be absurd, thanking my stars that I can unreservedly enjoy all fair things that are good of their kind. And so I told the inquirer this simple fact. If, in a mountainous country, varied, broken, studded with lakes, and rife with all the elements of the picturesque, you ascend some such superior elevation as this, you have, *looking downwards*, a striking panoramic scene, like this in its general features—more striking perhaps than beautiful, though this is all matter of taste. The difference lies herein. Here, you plunge your look downward, or sweep it over surrounding objects—and that's the end of it. In those other Alps, you add to the four or five or six thousand feet, below you, as much above—and it is that *upward* glance which takes in the marvels of glacier and snow-field and inaccessible peaks. My new acquaintance asked for no more comparisons, but let me enjoy myself in my own quiet way.

The walk down Mount Washington to Crawford's at the Great Notch, as I believe it is called, is rather a long affair. It must be ten miles, and parts of it are of the roughest. It took me four hours, in company with two intelligent and companionable young students of Harvard College, travelling (in the true way) a-foot, with knapsacks on their backs. But we hurried it too much, especially as the ridge over and along Mount Pleasant, and some of its fellows bearing Presidential names, abound in points of view worth dwelling on. Moreover I was foot-galled; and this reminds me that, inasmuch as I cannot to-day conclude my rambling reminiscences, I may as well wind up with a touch of information and of advice. The one is intended for the benefit of pedestrians who make excursions of this sort; the other for stay-at-homes in flat countries, who have no definite notion whatever of the ups and downs of hilly regions.

In the first place, then, you who walk are painfully aware that a sore foot is almost a calamity, if it befall you whilst *en route*. Remedy there is none; be thankful that there is an infallible preventive, of whose unfailing excellence I can speak with unreserved commendation. On its simple merits I once averaged in Switzerland twenty-five miles a day, for thirty successive days; and this without gall or blister. Fool that I was, to neglect it, two or three weeks ago. Nothing is easier. Ere you start in the morning, soap or grease the naked foot thoroughly, and then draw the stocking over it. Wash off, with a dash of brandy in the water, on finishing your day's work. The play of the foot is the preservative against abrasion—a certain one, I assure you.

In the second place, if—passing your life amid prairies or savannahs—you are sometimes puzzled to comprehend allusions to buttresses, shoulders, ridges, peaks, cones, ravines, and the various terms in use among enthusiastic mountaineers, I think I can put you on a very simple explanatory track. Next time you lie in bed, with a few spare moments for reflection upon this grave topic, just turn on to your back and elevate one knee or both knees. The coverlid or sheet will immediately assume—I am serious in saying—a curiously correct semblance, I might almost term it a model in relief, of the face of any mountainous country. Laugh not, but try it. A slight movement on your part varies the form and outline and relative bearing of hill and vale, raises a pinnacle here, or there sinks a gorge precipitously steep. If I had the misfortune to be confined to bed by sickness—excluding gout, which might render the process impossible—I could thus, with the aid of a map and some tables of distances, design a passable fac-simile of the leading White Mountains themselves. Why Yankee ingenuity should not long ago have manufactured *papier-maché* plans thereof, in relief, altogether passes my comprehension. They would sell well as souvenirs of travel.

SLIDING SCALE OF THE INCONSOLABLES.

From the French.

How rapid is the progress of oblivion, with respect to those who are no more! How many a quadrille shall we see, this winter, exclusively made up from the ranks of inconsolable widows! Widows of this order exist only in the literature of the tombstone. In the world, and after the lapse of a certain period, there is but one sort of widows inconsolable—those who refuse to be comforted, because they can't get married again!

One of our most distinguished sculptors was summoned, a short time since, to the house of a young lady, connected by birth with a family of the highest grade in the aristocracy of wealth, and united in marriage to the heir of a title illustrious in the military annals of the Empire.

The union, formed under the happiest auspices, had been, alas! of short duration. Death, unpitying death, had ruptured it, by prematurely carrying off the young husband. The sculptor was summoned by the widow.

He traversed apartments silent and deserted, until he was introduced into a bed-room, and found himself in presence of a lady, young and beautiful, but habited in the deepest mourning, and with a face furrowed by tears.

"You are aware," said she, with a painful effort and a voice half choked by sobs, "You are aware of the blow which I have received?"

The artist bowed, with an air of respectful condolence.

"Sir," continued the widow, "I am anxious to have a funeral monument erected, in honour of the husband whom I have lost."

The artist bowed again.

"I wish that the monument should be superb, worthy of the man whose loss I weep, proportioned to the unending grief into which his loss has plunged me. I care not what it costs. I am rich, and I will willingly sacrifice all my fortune to do honour to the memory of an adored husband. I must have a temple—with columns—in marble—and in the middle—on a pedestal—his statue."

"I will do my best to fulfill your wishes, Madam," replied the artist; "but I had not the honour of acquaintance with the deceased, and a likeness of him is indispensable for the due execution of my work. Without doubt, you have his portrait?"

The widow raised her arm, and pointed despairingly to a splendid likeness by

Amaury Duval.

"A most admirable picture!" observed the artist; "and the painter's name is sufficient guarantee for its striking resemblance to the original."

"Those are his very features, Sir; it is himself. It wants but life. Ah! Would that I could restore it to him at the cost of all my blood!"

"I will have this portrait carried to my studio, Madam, and I promise you that the marble shall reproduce it exactly."

The widow, at these words, sprung up, and at a single bound throwing herself towards the picture, with arms stretched out as though to defend it, exclaimed:

"Take away this portrait! carry off my only consolation! my sole remaining comfort! never! never!"

"But Madam, you will only be deprived of it for a short time, and—"

"Not an hour! not a minute! could I exist without his beloved image! Look you, Sir, I have had it placed here, in my own room, that my eyes might be fastened upon it, without ceasing, and through my tears. His portrait shall never leave this spot one single instant, and in contemplating that will I pass the remainder of a miserable and sorrowful existence."

"In that case, Madam, you will be compelled to permit me to take a copy of it. But do not be uneasy—I shall not have occasion to trouble your solitude for any length of time; one sketch—one sitting will suffice."

The widow agreed to this arrangement; she only insisted that the artist should come back the following day. She wanted him to set to work on the instant, so great was her longing to see the mausoleum erected. The sculptor, however, remarked that he had another work to finish first. This difficulty she sought to overcome by means of money.

"Impossible," replied the artist, "I have given my word; but do not distress yourself; I will apply to it so diligently, that the monument shall be finished in as short a time as any other sculptor would require, who could apply himself to it forthwith."

"You see my distress," said the widow; "you can make allowance for my impatience. Be speedy, then, and above all, be lavish of magnificence. Spare no expense; only let me have a masterpiece."

Several letters echoed these injunctions, during the few days immediately following the interview.

At the expiration of three months the artist called again. He found the widow still in weeds, but a little less pallid, and a little more coquettishly dressed in her mourning garb.

"Madam," said he, "I am entirely at your service."

"Ah! at last; this is fortunate," replied the widow, with a gracious smile.

"I have made my design, but I still want one sitting, for the likeness. Will you permit me to go into your bed-room?"

"Into my bed-room? For what?"

"To look at the portrait again."

"Oh! yes; have the goodness to walk into the drawing-room; you will find it there now."

"Ah!"

"Yes; it hangs better there; it is better lighted in the drawing-room, than in my own room."

"Would you like, Madam, to look at the design for the monument?"

"With pleasure. Oh! what a size! What profusion of decorations! Why, it is a palace, Sir, this tomb!"

"Did you not tell me, Madam, that nothing could be too magnificent? I have not considered the expense; and by the way, here is a memorandum of what the monument will cost you."

"Oh, Heavens!" exclaimed the widow, after having cast an eye over the total adding-up. "Why, this is enormous!"

"You begged me to spare no expense."

"Yes, no doubt, I desire to do things properly, but not exactly to make a fool of myself."

"This, at present, you see, is only a design; and there is time yet to cut it down."

"Well, then, suppose we were to leave out the temple, and the columns, and all the architectural part, and content ourselves with the statue? It seems to me that would be very appropriate."

"Certainly it would."

"So let it be, then—just the statue alone."

Shortly after this second visit, the sculptor fell desperately ill. He was compelled to give up work; but, on returning from a tour in Italy, prescribed by his physician, he presented himself once more before the widow, who was then in the tenth month of her mourning. He found, this time, a few roses among the cypress, and some smiling colours playing over half-shaded grounds.

The artist brought with him a little model of his statue, done in plaster, and offering in miniature the idea of what his work was to be.

"What do you think of the likeness?" he inquired of the widow.

"It seems to me a little flattered; my husband was all very well, no doubt; but you are making him an Apollo!"

"Really? well, then, I can correct my work by the portrait."

"Don't take the trouble—a little more, or less like, what does it matter?"

"Excuse me, but I am particular about likenesses."

"If you absolutely must—"

"It is in the drawing-room, yonder, is it not? I'll go in there."

"It is not there any longer," replied the widow, ringing the bell.

"Baptiste," said she to the servant who came in, "bring down the portrait of your master."

"The portrait that you sent up to the garret, last week, Madam?"

"Yes."

At this moment the door opened, and a young man of distinguished air entered; his manners were easy and familiar, he kissed the fair widow's hand, and tenderly inquired after her health.

"Who in the world is this good man in plaster?" asked he, pointing with his finger to the statuette, which the artist had placed upon the mantel-piece.

"It is the model of a statue for my husband's tomb."

"You are having a statue of him made? The devil it's very majestic!"

"Do you think so?"

"It is only great men who are thus cut out of marble, and at full length; it seems to me, too, that the deceased was a very ordinary personage."

"In fact, his bust would be sufficient."

"Just as you please, Madam," said the sculptor.

"Well, let it be a bust, that's—determined!"

Two months later, the artist, carrying the bust, encountered on the stairs a merry party. The widow, giving her hand to the elegant dandy who had caused the statue of the deceased to be cut down, was on his way to the Mayor's office, where she was about to take a second oath of conjugal fidelity.

If the bust had not been completed, it would willingly have been dispensed with. When, some time later, the artist called for his money, there was an outcry about the price; and it required very little less than a threat of legal proceedings, before the widow, consoled and remarried, concluded by resigning herself to pay for this funeral homage, reduced as it was, to the memory of her departed husband.

RAMBLING RECORDS.

THE GENTLE ARLESIANS.

**With one exception, however, I gleaned nothing of information that is not already chronicled in the guide-books; and that one piece of information I only set down, because I think it contains a hint that may be made practically useful in certain enterprising circles of New York.

We were in the Arena at Arles. It was a splendid day—barring the Mistral, that windy nuisance, which, as it eddied through the antique and ample Roman corridors, brought to my recollection certain North-Westers experienced on a fine March day in Union Square. In fact, it was far too cold for sentimentalizing or tracing measurements. But the guardian, it seemed, had not latterly had much chance of exercising his vocation, and his tongue was too nimble to be frozen. And so at it he went. Only, being himself more interested in certain proceedings that had lately taken place within a boarded fence that now encloses the arena, than in historical or legendary lore, his subject was by many centuries more fresh than the ruins whereon we stood, sunning ourselves and crouching out of the wind's way. Arles, it appeared, had been favoured with a bull fight, real Spanish matadors doing the beastly honours; but to the credit of the city, be it said, the spectacle was received with intense disapprobation. The gentle Provencals, whose tastes are more Italian than Spanish, could not brook the sport dear to their fair Empress who sets fashions in Paris. Indeed, the beauteous Eugénie, I fear, will hold them to be the merest milk-sops, for when the grand climax of a disembowelled horse was exhibited before them, the Arlesians, male and female—in place of shouts of triumphant approval—gave vent to loud cries of shame and execration, and in short hissed the Spanish heroes incontinently from the scene of their performance.

But what has all this to do with the future of New York, it may be asked by any reader of these rambling reminiscences. Stay, a moment; I am only at the commencement. I, too inquired if this were all. "By no means, Sir," was the reply. "We had then the real *courses aux taureaux*, and excellent they were." Now I must own that my notions of this branch of the tauromachia were somewhat indistinct. I knew it was not precisely the same thing as buffalo-hunting on the prairies, or as a steeple-chase in Warwickshire or Yorkshire; but I could not have defined it to save my life. "Perhaps, Monsieur, has never seen one" was the next appropriate suggestion, and it led very naturally to my enlightenment. Briefly, then, after the torture of the quadrupeds, and the indignant dismissal of the Spanish matadors, the young gentlemen of the town took the place of the latter, and began a diversion, which must have been infinitely amusing, and which, I humbly submit, might be adopted on a different soil. A lively young bull was turned into the arena, and was followed by a number of lively youths, armed only with light staves whereon fluttered blood-red pennons. The fun consists in provoking the excitable animal by the red flags thrust before his face, and eluding the consequences by a run, a dodge, or a jump. The fence, which was a barrier for the bull, could easily be vaulted by a nimble-footed youth—and none but such would venture upon the field. There was just enough danger to make the game piquant; scarcely enough to make it objectionable. One indiscreet young fellow did indeed narrowly escape a catastrophe on the occasion described to me; but the fault was entirely his own. He had been breakfasting at some Arlesian Delmonico's, and had partially lost his wits before coming to the encounter, while retaining all his courage. Therefore it happened—and I only tell the story as it was told me— that the youth, when pursued by the bull, tripped and fell, and the horns of the brute were immediately thrust into the fullest part of his peg-top trousers. A great sensation among the spectators! The bull succeeded in raising and throwing over his head the object of his attack, but by no means in disentangling himself therefrom. His frantic efforts to bring about a summary toss were for some minutes unsuccessful; and the reader may conceive the mingled sense of the ludicrous and the fearful, that pervaded the assembly. Finally—for even French cassimere will give way in the end—he, the bull that is, achieved his aim, and threw his unconscious tormentor a summerset, being diverted from ulterior measures of vengeance by fresh attacks made upon him, while the crest-fallen hero of the adventure was promptly bundled over the paling. To sum up this sketch of the sport, in the humane and pithy words of the guardian of the Amphitheatre—"it does no harm whatever to the bull, and very little to the young gentleman."

Now then, Mr. Niblo; why should you not establish a Tauro-drome in the centre of civilization? The leaning of the day is toward athletic exercise. In England, at present, there is a run upon rifle-corps; and the boldest riders are all bent upon becoming the crackest shots. In New York, I have read since my absence in Europe, that the great English Eleven have begotten a very rage for cricket. An excellent move this; but then the climate is against it, and the summer is short, and the game is utterly incomprehensible to the gentler sex, who are always prompt to encourage the manly prowess of their admirers. Besides, for lack of a permanent Bude light of adequate strength, we have not yet achieved the desideratum of playing cricket during those special hours when the youth of a commercial community finds itself prone to relaxation. The *courses aux taureaux* might just as well take place by gas-light and in a New York circus, as amid Roman ruins and under the blaze of sunshine. The dandies of Broadway have the two main requisites for brilliant success in this suggested entertainment. Their pluck may not be doubted; and who that has seen them, agile and unwearied in the German or the *valse à deux temps*, could question their ability to outfoot the fleetest bull that Andalusia itself could supply? I commend the matter then to the serious consideration of Managers in search of novelties, and to belles who would discover what stuff their beaux are made of.

AT NUREMBURG.

For these thirty-eight years past, the *Albion* hath been protesting once a week, in the Latin tongue, that they who skip over the water change only their sky, not their mental existence. Nor did I ever doubt—indeed I ought to have faith therein—the truth of this motto, until I found myself yesterday in one of the streets of this old city of Nuremburg, with no promenaders at the moment save myself. There was not a man in sight, tiled with a black beaver chimney- pot; nor a woman redolent of the Rue de la Paix or Regent Street. Then it was that I incontinently asked myself if I were truly a Briton by birth and an Anglo-American by local ties; or whether I were not in fact a German burgher of the middle ages. I should scarcely have been surprised at sight of grave Albert Durer himself coming round the corner, or at hearing Hans Sachs, the cobbler poet, trolling one of his six thousand ditties.

To say this, is simply to add the testimony of another witness to that which has set down Nuremburg as the city of all Europe least changed with changing times. The very little that has been done of late years in the way of repairing and rebuilding, within the walls, has been done in strict accordance with the prevalent mediæval style. The result is that—whereas elsewhere, when you stumble upon a private dwelling of moderate proportions showing plainly that it was built some two or three or four or five centuries ago, you congratulate yourself upon having discovered a curiosity (as such a one really would be in Paris, for instance)—here the difficult search would be for a house, modern and spruce. Not that a rectangularly-ornamented gable-end is the quintessence of architectural beauty, or that a basement front of low iron- barred windows suggests an agreeable or hospitable interior. By no means. If this were all, there would be considerable quaintness, and nought beyond. But it is otherwise. Some of the decorative bits that catch the eye right and left, are absolute gems in their way—whether oriel windows, or fantastic turrets, or figures and devices embossed and sculptured. Taste, generally for the Gothic, but diverging at a later date into the Renaissance style, seems to have run riot here in wilful playfulness.

Of the regular sights set down in the hand-books, and explored by conscientious Englishmen with their Murrays under their arms, it would not be appropriate to speak at length. I may however indulge in an allusion to the different material, whereof are constructed two of the most highly-laboured marvels, here exhibited. Now the city itself is divided into two nearly equal parts by the small river Pegnitz, these parts bearing the names respectively of the principal church that stands in either. The one is dedicated to St. Sebald, the other to St. Lawrence. The former, as its chief curiosity, contains the shrine of its patron Saint, an elaborate and most exquisitely wrought fretwork canopy, about fifteen feet in height, beneath which repose his remains. The design is in a measure architectural, and Gothic of course; but the ornamentation is its great glory, though one is staggered somewhat at the irreverent juxtaposition of the twelve Apostles with Cupids and Mermaids, and at sundry Fathers of the Church disporting themselves amid clusters of fruit and bouquets of flowers. This monument of artistic skill was the work of Peter Vischer, one of the worthies of Nuremburg, and has been completed three hundred and forty years. The able worker, having dispensed with consistency in the admixture of Christian and Pagan accessories, as I have mentioned, was at least justified in introducing a figure of himself as one of the human animals; and a very fine statuette he makes, with chisel in hand and his working apron about him. Now mark, if you please, O attentive reader, this shrine of St. Sebald is entirely cast in bronze. To say that the effect is beautiful, is too limited praise. It is harmonious; thoroughly satisfying to the eye; perfect.

Cross with me now, if you be not weary, one of the dozen picturesque bridges over the Pegnitz, and let us see what Adam Krafft, another great Nuremburger of that same age, has done in the same line of Gothic decoration for the Church of St. Lawrence. His work is a shrine, or I should rather say a repository for the sacramental wafer of the Roman Catholic rite. It is an open- work spire, tapering to the height of sixty feet, with an infinity of graceful detail, and rare sculptures in high and low relief. One fantasy is, I think, unique of its kind. The roof is a little too low to admit the crowning summit fairly; and the top, therefore, has been made to bend over. The effect— purposely designed, I cannot doubt—is odd; nor can I agree with the fantastic remark of Murray's Handbook, that it "has the air of a plant which is chocked in its further growth." Spires and plants are not endowed with equal pliability, and the idea of one of the former waving about, or nodding gracefully, suggests an immediate "stand from under." And this all the more in this instance, because—which brings me thus round-aboutedly to my main point
—the material hereon employed is stone, a clean and white-toned stone, that looks as though its excellent carvings and mouldings had been completed only for the last Crystal Palace Exhibition. The apparent newness is downright provoking; and if Adam Krafft could peep at it from his honoured

grave, he would never dream that he has lain therein three centuries and a half. Let me say further—having thus stumbled upon personalities—that he too made himself as durable as his work. And with more modesty than Master Peter Vischer above named, who moulded for himself a niche in his monument corresponding, in size and position, to the one assigned to the patron Saint, though being at the opposite end of the shrine, the glorifier and the glorified could not be taken into one glance and a comparison forced. There was more modesty, I say, in Adam Krafft's mode of travelling down the stream of Time as showman of his show, though he was not methinks without a dash of *craft*, as befits the bearer of his name. Down upon their marrow- bones (as the school boys have it) with rounded backs grope Adam and his two apprentices, the three backs forming a base of operations, or in plainer words upholding the sixty-feet structure, and doing for it that which is done beneath his rival's shrine by a snail at each of the four corners. Perhaps, after all, the sculptor-architect was wiser than the bronze-caster, in his mode of identifying himself with his work. Amid a multitude of figures and emblems, Peter Vischer, as well as St. Sebald, may be overlooked, for they are small in size; but you can scarcely avoid asking "who are these three?" when you note how lofty is the edifice that the large quasi-Atlases bear.

Enough, touching these minor differences. The essential one, whereof I intended to speak, is the material in which the pair wrought respectively. I have said that the bronze entirely satisfied my critical eye, which is tantamount to saying that it charmed me. Not so with the stone. It is obviously ill-adapted for detached ornamentation, needing the solid adjunct of buttress, window, wall, or pillar, just as ivy needs the oak, or (may I utter such a term?) lace the woman. Indeed, with all my admiration for sundry mediæval specimens of Gothic architecture, wherein I scarcely yield to John Ruskin himself, I confess that the famous Eleanor's Crosses in England never quite pleased me, because therein the tracery and dainty delicacies of the design are not backed by anything massive. The greater part of my readers will not agree with me. I am sorry, but can't help it. Only, I don't want to see any more open-work baskets in stone. Give me the most fantastical of Gothic devices, as many as you please, so long as they have something to cling to.

Finally, I have fallen quite in love with this quaint, irregular old place. Nor do I know how long I might have loitered, had not the inevitable disillusion come, as come it will over so many promising things and fair. Otherwise I might have gone back—in imagination—to those honest old times of Durer, Vischer, Krafft, and Company, and imagined myself a free burgher of a free city. But the spell was doubly broken. At the old castle—whereof some small apartments are unpretendingly fitted up for the King and Queen of Bavaria—there comes upon one, in another part thereof, a vision of certain instruments of torture, used undoubtedly in those good old times to keep the burghers submissive to their oligarchy of merchant princes. And again at the Rath- haus, or Hotel de Ville; the maidenly show-woman lighted us by lanthorn- light through a set of subterranean dungeons, too numerous to have been destined for offenders only against the criminal laws, too horrible to be sanctioned under our creed of comparative gentleness. And so, on the whole, I returned back to actual existence, and to all the boredom of Parliamentary conflicts and Presidential elections, with a certain sense of relief.

ROMAN NOMENCLATURE.

By dint of many rambles I am become fairly versed in the topography of Rome; but its history, as elucidated by monuments or relics, is a perpetual riddle to the beholder. The Republic, the Empire, the Barbarian Invasions, Free Lances, Barons, Kings, and Popes—all are suggested; all come before you in confused array; not unfrequently, three or four at once. You shall go into a church to hear mass amid modern tawdriness, entering through a mediæval porch, taking your place between walls that were put up long before the Christian era, and under a roof supported by pillars whereon the sun of Phrygia has shone. Pagan and Christian—all is jumbled; until finally, unless you have the patience of Job and the zeal of an antiquarian, you begin to doubt all legendary and historic lore, and to measure what you see by its external attractiveness alone. One thing, however, is clearly marked. You are groping about, in a state of vexed uncertainty; suddenly you come upon an inscription, conspicuous, in large legible letters, often gilded. Now you are grateful. You stride up; and lo, there stands, emblazoned before you the interesting fact that such or such a Pontifex Maximus, some Benedict, or Clemens, or Pius, or Leo, or Gregory, restored, excavated, ornamented, or built, as the case may have been, the object upon which you have been pondering. Neither, in the dearth of desirable information, are you compensated by the opportunity of picking up chronological knowledge in regard to the Papacy. These fulsome records omit, not only all description that might be useful; they fail to mention the year of the World, or the year of Grace, altogether. In place thereof, you learn that the digging or decoration in question took place in a certain year of the reign of a certain Pope; but as the chair of St. Peter has had one hundred and sixteen occupants, between A.D. 1000 and A.D. 1860, "Anno VI. of Innocent VI." or "Anno II. of Julius II." does not materially aid the memory as to dates. This petty craving after chiselled or painted immortality is nowhere more contemptibly exhibited than in Raphael's famous Loggie at the Vatican, where, over each separate window, one reads in staring type, "Leo X., Pontifex Maximus." Surely there is something strangely inconsistent, in a power that boasts its remote origin and its endowment in perpetuity, thus taking infinite pains to isolate its historical fragments.

A smile only—not a grunt of indignation—is elicited by another peculiarity of Rome, which comes under the lounger's notice. Something of the same sort is perhaps also observable in all large cities; but it never struck me so strongly. I allude to the names of the streets and squares and public places, which names by the way are carefully and prominently labelled. The jumble is curious, though one starts a little at times from what to Protestant eyes seems irreverent. Take a sample, dispensing with the titles in Italian. You may stroll through the street of the Three Virgins, of the Three Robbers, of Jesus, of the Tarpeian Rock, of the Two Butchers' Shops, of the Baboon, of Divine Love, of the New Benches, of the Prefects, of the House-tops, of Jesus and Mary, of the Greeks, of the Tower of Blood, of the Triton, of the Guardian Angel, of the Strumpet, of the Soul, of the Scrofula, of the Eagle, of the Lion's Mouth, of the Five Moons, of Minerva, of the Incurables, of the Wind, of the Wolf, of St. John Beheaded. You may halt in the square of the Mouth of Truth, in that of the Field of Flowers, in that of the Satyrs, in that of Consolation, in that of the Goose. It is evident that no ruling mind or principle has regulated this public nomenclature. *Tot homines, quot sententiæ.*

And is it not the same thing in private affairs? What variety of tastes! Here is a specimen. Two young men of my acquaintance, who have been campaigning in India, arrived here, the other day, on their first visit. One of them had a relative here, of a scholastic turn of mind, who was bringing a protracted sojourn to a close; and to him the cavalry officers were in a measure consigned. "Can you tell me what's to be seen at Ostia and Veii?" said one of them to me, forty-eight hours after their arrival. "Our friend, B., is going to take us a day's excursion to each place, to-morrow and the following day." I could scarcely keep my countenance. The poor innocents were sold to an antiquarian. Ostia is destitute of any objects that would repay a half-hour's walk. As for Veii, the learned have only agreed of late whereabouts that ancient city stood.

BRIGANDS, BEGGARS, AND SOUVENIRS.

My last communication was from Rome. It was piquant, on the day of departure thence from Naples, to dine at Terracina with a Prussian family, who had been stopped and robbed by brigands, at eight o'clock the previous morning, at a spot between Velletri and Cisterna. There was however no *Fra Diavolo* in the case. The respectable *père de famille*, who with his sons and daughters had been laid under contribution, informed us that the fellows were evidently peasants unused to the trade; that they presented guns, in exacting their demand for money; but that they were nervous in their brief operation, and that they did not ransack the trunks, nor even carry off the watches and rings of the party. The chief sufferer was the vetturino, whom fright and the loss of thirty-six dollars had thrown into a fever. causing the detention which brought us into contact with the narrators. We passed on our way, without adventure; the safest period, there as elsewhere, being that which immediately follows one. I incline to think that extreme destitution induced this recourse to a practice almost obsolete, as it probably gave rise to the personal robberies, unattended with violence, which have been recently rife in Rome itself.

And in connection with this point, I may swell the laments of late travellers as to the chronic prevalence, throughout Southern Italy, of those other unceasing robberies of extortion and mendicancy, which are so much more difficult of toleration. I declare that of all the mythical personages of classic lore brought back to one's memory by local association, whether in the Elysian Fields or on the borders of Lake Avernus, the Harpies are those who alone survive, and who obtrude themselves always and everywhere, in season and out of season. The foul brood have assumed human semblance, and haunt you in all varieties. The unbidden cicerone, or the sturdy beggar—it is hard to say which is the worse.

How I anathematized them both at Sorrento, where there are certain souvenirs of Tasso, not so direct and tangible as those preserved in the Convent of San Onofrio at Rome, but which are worth the tracing. You will remember that the hapless poet found a resting place here in the house of his sister, after he escaped from his seven years' imprisonment at Ferrara. To be adjured, for charity, in the name of the Virgin and every Saint in the calendar—to have a jackass and a guide, or a jackass of a guide, thrust upon you, *nolens volens* for an excursion that you have no mind to take, or to be importuned to "put out, put out, put out to sea," when you know that March winds and waves make the azure grotto of Capri totally inaccessible—these diversions, I say, do not assist one in gathering up one's reminiscences of Tasso, however much they may chasten and so improve the temper.

And here I may observe also upon a peculiarity that marks the research of certain travellers, somewhat akin perhaps to the taste which induces certain readers to trace history through personal memoirs. in place of studying broader narrations. If truth were told, there are a hundred who commune with Pepys and Horace Walpole, to ten who find delight in Hume. So is it—though by no means in the same proportion—with sight-seers on ground that is rich in historical associations. All their sympathies, or the larger portion of them at least, are with individuals, as though there were no grappling with a race, a nation, an age that is past. Stories, wholly or in part fictitious, are their hand-books. To them the Capitol of Rome is the scene of Rienzi's rise and fall, as interpreted by Bulwer Lytton. At Pompeii their chief care is to find out the abode of Glaucus and Ione. Nor can it be denied that there is an additional charm in this mode of viewing localities that are new to us, if it be not the most philosophical. In my own case, without needless parading of the degree in which I share this gentle weakness or disapprove it, I must own that its exercise gives at times an unexpected zest to a ramble. Whilst in Rome, for instance, I do not think that one's serious views of history or art are in any manner jarred upon, because here and there one stumbles upon relics that savour of individuality. At any rate I should not like to have missed the old mansion of the Anviti family, near the bridge of St. Angelo, mentioned by that old gossip, Benvenuto Cellini, as the frequent rendezvous of Michael Angelo, Raffaele, Cardinal Bembo, and other choice spirits of his day. I should have been sorry to have omitted a visit to the boudoir of Lucrezia Borgia, in the Convent close beside the church of St. Pietro in Vincolo, once the residence of Pope Alexander VI., and now mainly converted into a barrack for the troops of "the elder son of the Church." The part however in which is placed this small apartment, decorated with frescoes of the period, is still applied to conventual purposes. There is no legend about the matter, at least so far as regards the possession of the Borgia family; and the room being small in size, and unique in situation and style of ornament within and without, it is not difficult to believe that it was the chosen resort of a young lady in days when there was less gadding about than now. Still, to be candid, I must own that in musing here, as in looking at the lock of the same amiable woman's hair preserved in the Ambrosian Library of Milan, one is apt to have one's recollections of mediæval depravity not slightly tinctured by visions of Giulia Grisi in the prime of her voice and beauty, to say nothing of Victor Hugo's grand drama, and old Mademoiselle Georges' unrivalled performance therein.

Again, and lastly—lest the reader imagine that when once I get back to Rome, I am spell-bound and cannot leave it—what traveller has not cast a pleased eye upwards towards the window whence the baker's daughter, A. D. 1515, or thereabouts, ogled the young prince of painters as he passed by on his way to, or from his work, at the Farnesina Palace? You know the precise spot, O Viator, in a small piazza very near the Ponte Sisto? The house is white- washed or yellow-washed now; but there is the old Ionic pilaster, yet embedded in the wall, and the ornamental architectural mouldings yet shut in the Fornarina's window. And here it occurs to me to make one more digression, for the purpose of suggesting a theory of my own touching one of the many portraits of La Fornarina that have come down to us, and that vary so much in expression though all evidently intended for the same person. Between the fine one in the Tribune at Florence, and the filthy one in the Sciarra Palace at Rome, there is the widest possible difference. The former is evidently enough a woman unrefined, though beautiful; but there is neither coarseness nor indelicacy in the portraiture. The latter has both these characteristics, pushed to an extreme that is repulsive. It is said to be a copy from Raffaele by Giulio Romano. Now my belief is, that it was painted as a quiz upon his master's grace and delicacy, by the scapegrace pupil who ran counter to those special attributes. Meretricious, ugly, and vulgar, this wretched creature bears emblasoned in large letters on the bracelet upon her arm the name of Raffaele Sanzio d'Urbino. This piece of impudence seems to me the crowning touch. I can't credit that such a Fornarina ever came from Raffaele's easel. I do think that a coarse-minded and coarse-handed young artist may have made fun of his superior in oil—as modern literary wags have sometimes done in ink—and that Raffaele therefore is in no way answerable for that caricature in the Sciarra, which affects to be a reproduction from himself.

LIVRES DES VOYAGEURS.

Verily there is no lack of the plainer symbols of humanity, to remind the wanderer that Childe Harold was bitterly truthful, when he appended to his inimitable descriptions of the Alps the assertion that they

"serve to show,
How Earth may pierce to Heaven, yet leave vain man below."

The impertinences and follies that are penned by men and women in the various Livres des Voyageurs, wherein they record their names, were alone sufficient proof of this. It is true that enthusiasm and fine feeling cannot endure for an indefinite period; and that he would be a sorry companion who always brought his stilts to the dinner-table. Still, one must regret that a certain craving for notoriety seems to impel so many a tourist to write himself down an ass, whilst no sense of fairness restrains others from commenting, appropriately or inappropriately, upon the names or remarks of predecessors. There is a cowardice and cruelty herein which has, I confess, sometimes made me angry, when the identity, characters, and conduct of the individuals concerned were alike unknown or indifferent to me. In place, however, of prolonging this digression, and without the least notion of proving anything whatever by the citation, I beg to offer the reader a brace of extracts from the visitors' record book at the Montanvert.

The first tickled me exceedingly, as a genuine specimen of the so-called Irish Bull. Mr. Somebody had entered his name, and added thereto this valuable bit of information: "Walked up from Chamouni in four hours and a-half, *having lost the greater part of his way?*" The italics are mine, of course; but is not the *mot* worth its space in print?

My other extract concerns some of my young countrywomen, and I trust that their countrywomen who may read it will forgive me for putting it into circulation. They are very poor laughers, who never laugh when the joke tells against themselves; in this instance it is we who pay the piper. A party of English school girls had been lately at Montanvert with their governess, and had set down their names one after another in the big book, as is the custom there. A waggish Frenchman, waiting of course until their backs were turned, had bracketted the list, and written against the conclave this pithy and caustic criticism: *"Teint rouge; appétit géant; langage embarrassé."* What an ungallant scamp! Yet it must be owned that the same absurd album is rich in provocatives. A running fire of sarcasm, exchanged between English and French tourists, marks almost every page.

A SINGULAR ANAGRAM.

Among the curiosities—not of literature—but of letters, the Anagram was wont to be a favourite in the days of a by-gone generation. Who, for instance, has not smiled blandly over that famous transposition, which aptly converts "Horatio Nelson" into *Honor est à Nilo*?

The taste, however, for this sort of laborious trifling has almost passed away; nor do we propose to re-open the subject of cabalistic lettering. Our only purport is to offer a new specimen of its eccentricities, which came upon us recently during a vain attempt to solve certain mysteries, that occupy just now many serious minds. It is commended alike to snappers-up of unconsidered trifles, and to readers who chance to be imbued with a little tinge of superstitious sensitiveness. We strive to hope that, though almost as curious, it is not so unimpeachably appropriate as the one quoted above. The name, so much in men's mouths, "Louis Napoleon Bonaparte," may by this method be converted into, *An open plot—arouse, Albion*!

A WELL KNOWN DOCUMENT,

Very Slightly Paraphrased.

A comparison of the following lines, with the original American Declaration of Independence, will show that the earnest and impassioned language of real life is sometimes closely assimilated to blank verse.

When, in their course, human events compel
One people to dissolve the social bands
That linked them with another, and to take
Among the powers of the Earth that station,
Equal and separate, to which the laws
Of Nature and of Nature's God, by right,
Entitle them—respect to the opinions
Of fellow men calls on them to declare
The causes, which have rendered necessary
Such separation.
       We, then, hold these truths
To be self-evident: That all mankind
Are equal, and endowed by theirCreator
With certain unalienable rights:
That amongst these are Life, and Liberty,
And the Pursuit of Happiness: That men,
To make these rights available and safe,
Have instituted Governments, deriving
Their lawful power from the freeconsent

Of those they govern: That when anyform
Of Government is proved to bedestructive
Of these their ends, it is the People's right
To alter, or abolish it, and found
A Government anew, with principles
So laid for its foundation, and with powers
In such form organized, as shall to them
Seem most conducive to their happiness
And safety.
      Prudence will, indeed, dictate
That long-established Governments should not
Be changed for any light or transient cause:

And all experience, accordingly,
Hath shown that men are more disposed to suffer,
So long as evils are endurable,
Than to assert their rights, and throw aside
Their customary forms. But when abuses
And usurpations, in a lengthened train,
Pursue an object steadfastly, evincing
A firm design to bow them down beneath
Absolute despotism, it is their right,
It is their bounden duty, to throw off
Such Government, and to provide new guards
For their security in future.

                                                        Such

Has been the patient sufferance of these
Our Colonies, and such is now the need,
That forces them to change their present systems
Of Government. Great Britain's present King
Hath made his history the history
Of usurpation, and of injuries
Often repeated, and directly tending
To the establishment of Tyranny

Over these States: to prove this, let the World
In candour listen to undoubted facts.
    He has refused to give assent to laws,
Wholesome, and needful for the public good.
He has denied his Governors the power
To sanction laws of pressing urgency,
Unless suspended in their operation,
Till his assent should be obtained; and when
Suspended thus, he has failed wilfully
To give them further thought. He has refused
To sanction other laws, deemed advantageous
To districts thickly peopled, unless they,
Who dwelt therein, would basely throw away
Their right to representatives—a right
Inestimable, to themselves and only
To Tyrants formidable. In the hope
To weary them into a weak compliance
With his obnoxious measures, he has summoned
The Legislative Bodies to assemble
At places inconvenient, and unusual,

And whence their public records were remote.
He has repeatedly dissolved the Houses
Of Representatives for interfering
With manly firmness, when he has invaded
The People's rights. Long time he has refused,
After such dissolutions, to convene
Others in lieu of them; whereby, the powers
Of Legislation, since they might not be
Annihilated, have for exercise
Been forced upon the body of the people;
Leaving, meanwhile, the unprotected State
To dangers of invasion from without,
And inward anarchy. He has endeavoured

To check the population of these States,
Thwarting the laws for naturalization
Of foreigners, withholding his assent
From other laws, that might encourage them
In immigrating hither, and enhancing
The price of new allotments of the soil.
    He has obstructed the administration
Of Justice, by his veto on the laws
Establishing judiciary powers
He has made Judges on his will alone
Dependent, for the tenure of their office,
For the amount, and for the proper payment
Of their emoluments. He has erected
New offices in multitudes, and sent
Swarms of his officers to harass us,
And to eat out our substance. He has kept,
In times of peace, among us, standing armies,
Without the sanction of our Legislatures.
His aim has been to place the military
Above the civil power, and beyond
Its just control. He has combined with others
To make us subject to a jurisdiction,
In spirit foreign to our Constitution,
And unacknowledged by our laws; assenting
To acts, that they have passed with semblance only
Of legislation: Acts for quartering
Among us bodies of armed troops: For shielding,
By a mock trial, those their instruments

From punishment for any murders done
On our inhabitants: For cutting off
Our trade with every quarter of the world—
For laying on us taxes not approved
By our consent: For oft-times robbing us

Of any benefit that might attend
Trial by jury: For transporting us
Beyond the seas, to answer for offences,
Imputed to us: For abolishing,
Within a neighbouring province, the free system
Of English laws; establishing therein
An arbitrary power; and enlarging
Its boundaries, to render it at once
The fit example, and the instrument
For bringing into these our Colonies
The same despotic rule: For taking from us
Our Charters; and abolishing our laws
Most valued; changing thus, in principle,
Our forms of Government: And for suspending
Our Legislatures, with the declaration
That they, themselves, in each and every case,
Were vested with supreme authority
To legislate for us.
                              He has laid down
His sway, by holding us without the pale
Of his protection, and by waging war
Against us. He has plundered on our seas;
Ravaged our coasts; our cities burnt; and taken
Our people's lives. He is transporting hither
Armies composed of foreign mercenaries,
To end the works of death, and desolation,
And tyranny, begun with circumstances
Of cruelty and perfidy unequalled
In the most barbarous ages, and unworthy
The Ruler of a nation civilized.
He has constrained our fellow-citizens,
On the high seas made captive, to bear arms
Against their country, and of friends and brothers

To be the executioners, or fall
Beneath his creatures' hands. He has excited

Amongst ourselves domestic insurrection;
And sought to bring on the inhabitants
Of our frontier the savage Indian,
Whose code of warfare, merciless and sure,
Spares not, in undistinguished massacre,
Age, sex, condition.
                              We, in every stage
Of these oppressions, have in humblest terms
Petitioned for redress. To our petitions,
Though oft repeated, there has been *one* answer—
Repeated injury.
                              A prince, whose life
And conduct thus are marked by every act
That may define a Tyrant, is unfit
To rule o'er Freemen.
                              Neither have we fa_led
In due attention to our British brethren.
From time to time, we have admonished them
Of efforts, by their Legislature made,
Unwarrantably to extend to us
Their jurisdiction. How we emigrated,
And settled here, we have reminded them.
We to their native justice have appealed
And magnanimity; and have conjured them,
By common kindred ties, to disavow
These usurpations, which, inevitably,
Would mar our intercourse and friendship. They
Have also turned a deaf ear to the voice
Of Justice and of Consanguinity.
So must we yield to the necessity
Which forces us to separate, and hold them—

As we do hold the rest of human kind—
Our enemies in War, in Peace our friends.
    We, therefore, who are here to represent
The States United of America,
In General Congress met, for rectitude
Of our intentions to the Judge Supreme
Of all things here in confidence appealing,
Do, in the name, and by authority
Of the good people of these Colonies,
Solemnly publish and declare, that these

United Colonies are, and of right
Ought to be, Free and Independent States:
That from allegiance to the British Crown
They are absolved: That all connecting ties
Of policy between them and Great Britain
Are, as they should be, totally dissolved:
And that, as Free and Independent States,
They have full power to levy war, conclude
Peace, and contract alliances, establish
Commerce, and do all other acts and things
Which Independent States of right may do.
  This is our Declaration: to support it,
With firm reliance on Divine protection,
We to each other mutually pledge
Our lives, our fortunes, and our sacred honour.

BEL PIEDE.

Browning, whose household gods were planted
  Beside the banks of classic Arno,
Once, in a dainty ballad, chanted
  The lady of the *bella mano*.

Pass from the Arno to the Tiber,
  From Tuscan to a Roman lady;
And let a humbler bard describe her—
  This fair one of the *bel piede*.

To Roman dame, as I and you know,
  Is rarely given a foot symmetrical;
No Cinderellas—many a Juno—
  Upon the Pincian we can yet recall.

Those were the days when bonnets did not
  Expose the face to every starer;
When skirts, worn short and airy, hid not
  The foot and ankle of the wearer.

With high arched instep, narrow, tapering,
  Divinely booted—none could beat hers—
The foot, that set my young heart capering,
  Came down the broad steps of St. Peter's.

Her long black veil, the crowd around me,
  Her swift landau, my swift emotion—
She came: her fairy foot spell-bound me;
  She went: which way, I had no notion.

Haunting all public haunts was fruitless,
  Mid solemn pomps, on festal hey-day;
Search for those glorious boots was bootless:
  Rome showed no more my *bel piede*.

In Paris next enchained it held me,
  Through redowa, waltz, all sorts of dances;
But mask and domino repelled me—

She moved, but I made no advances.

Again she passed—no trace behind her—
    I sought, enquired, left nothing undone;
But all was vain: I could not find her,
    And, in despair, set off for London.

The sea between Boulogne and Dover
    Was, as it always is, terrific;
Against that awful passage over,
    Why not invent some smooth specific?

Cloaked, muffled, shawled, a form was leaning
    Across the gunwale, keeping shady;
I recked not what might be its meaning—
    I thought not, then, of *bel piede*.

Sudden, a lurch, a shriek, a splashing!
    I knew the shriek was from a lady;
But horror through my brain went crashing—
    I saw, heels up, my *bel piede*!

She sank. No more! But O ye mermaids,
    Of whose long tails we've had a surfeit,
If ye were worthy to be her maids,
    You'd cut your tails, and copy her feet!

———————————————

WHO IS HE?

A Reply to Quevedo.

These lines were suggested by some sprightly verses, entitled "Who is She?" that had recently appeared in *Fraser's Magazine.*

A Spanish writer once decided,
    In flippant song,
That woman's lip, or tongue, or eye did
    All that went wrong.
Nay, that the true mode of unmasking
    Her wiles would be,
On all occasions simply asking—
    Pray, who is she?

Now, why must woman's petticoats
    Aye be the blamables?
How is't Quevedo never quotes
    Mankind's unnamables?
He rates the sex, and certès for it he
    Makes a good plea;
But can't I, on as good authority,
    Ask, who is he?

Quevedo swears that Eve and Helen
    Wrought dire mishaps:
That Adam and the Trojans fell in
    Their deep-laid traps.
Eve?—why Diabolus beguiled her;
    You know't, Quevedo!
Helen?—that rascal Paris wiled her:
    That's Homer's *credo*!

Trust me, man causes woman's failing;
    And, on my life,
He's always wantonly assailing
    Maid, widow, wife.
Beneath the surface let the gazer
    Look deep—he'll see

Some stronger vessel that betrays her:
  Just ask—who's he?

Is it a milk-maid drops her pailful?—
  Lubin's love-making:
Is her fate scandalous or baleful?—
  Lubin's been raking!
The school-girl loaths her bread and butter,
  Pouts o'er her tea,
Mumbles her lessons in a flutter—
  Ask, who is he?

Despite experience, what can set
  The widow hoping?
Why are wives sometimes gaddingmet,
  And sometimes moping?
Don't talk of widows' amorous bump,
  Of wives too free;
But pop the question to them, plump—
  Pray, who is he?

We're mighty prompt to throw the blame on
  The weaker fair sex;
When justice ought to fix the shame on
  Ours—not on their sex.
Ours the seduction and the fooling,
  If such there be:
Come; your exception to this ruling—
  Pray, who is he?

The old and hump-backed ply theirbattery
  Of gold and jewels;
Well-knit young fellows deal in flattery,
  Dance, song, oaths, duels.
So, to conclude, I'll take my oath, sir,
  Upon the Bible,
That to blame one—in place of both, sir,—
  Is a gross libel!

TO NINON.

From the French of Alfred de Musset.

Were I to tell thee, ne'ertheless, that, troth, I love thee well,
Blue-eyed brunette, blue-eyed brunette, thine answer who could tell?
Love is the cause of many a pang—their source thou well can'st guess;
No pity in him dwells, as thou must needs thyself confess:
And yet, ah! me, thou would'st perchance chastise me ne'ertheless!

Were I to tell thee that, beneath six months of silence crushed,
Long-hidden torments I have borne, and vows insensate hushed;
Ninon, despite thy careless air, thou hast a searching eye,
That, like a Fairy's, ere it come, what's coming can espy:
"I know it all, I know it all," thou would'st perchance reply.

Were I to tell thee that I roam in sweet, delirious dream,
Haunting thy footsteps so that I thy very shadow seem;
A tinge of sadness on thy cheek, a quick, mistrustful glance,—
Ninon, thou knowest well that these thy loveliness enhance: And
thus, that thou believest not, thou would'st reply perchance.

Were I to tell thee that my soul hoards up the lightest word,
That falling from thy lips at eve in our discourse I've heard;
Lady, thou know'st that, when aroused to anger or disdain,
Eyes, though of azure they may be, can still their lightnings rain:
And thine perchance would flashing say, "We must not meet again!"

Were I to tell thee that by night I wake and think of thee,
And that by day for thee I pray, and weep on bended knee,
Ah! Ninon, when thou laugh'st, the bee, as well thou art aware,
In hovering round thy rosy mouth, that 'twas a flower might swear:
Were I to tell thee all, perchance the laugh would still be there

But nothing shalt thou know of this. I venture, all untold,
Calmly to sit beneath thy lamp, and converse with thee hold.
I hear the murmur of thy voice, thy balmy breath inhale;
And thou may'st doubt me, or surmise, or laugh, I shall not quail;
Thine eyes shall see no cause in me, their kindly look to veil.

By stealth at times, in secret joy, mysterious flowers I glean,

When o'er thy harpsichord at eve enraptured I can lean,
And list from thy harmonious hands what fairy accents flow;
Or in voluptuous waltz, as round with flying feet we go,
I feel thee in mine arms, a reed, that's waving to and fro.

When from thy side I have been kept by thronged saloons at night,
And in my chamber draw my bolt that shuts the world from sight,
A thousand reminiscences I seize upon, and hold
In jealous grasp; and there, alone, like miser o'er his gold,
To Heaven my heart, all full of thee, with greedy joy unfold.

I love; and I have learned to speak in cool and careless tone.
I love; nought tells of it. I love; who knows it?—I alone!
Dear is my secret, dear the pain with which I am oppressed;
And I have sworn to love, without a hope on which to rest;
But not without a taste of joy—I see thee, and am blest.

No! not for me! I was not born such bliss supreme to meet:
To die within thy arms, or live contented at thy feet.
Alas! all proves it—e'en the grief that fain I would dispel.
Were I to tell thee, ne'ertheless, that, troth, I love thee well:
Blue-eyed brunette, blue-eyed brunette, thine answer who could tell?

THE LAST OF THE ROMAN GLADIATORS.

The incident, which the following stanzas attempt to describe, is historical. It is related by Gibbon in his "Decline and Fall of the Roman Empire."

Ye, who have the ruins seen
   Of the Coliseum's walls,
Think ye, what the sight hath been
   Of Rome's highest festivals!
If your fancy can restore
Crumbled arch and corridor,
         Call forth the dead;
Bid them fill again the seats,
Where now Echo only greets
       The stranger's tread.

Fourteen hundred years are past,
   Rome hath fallen in her pride,
Since the gladiator last
   In the Coliseum died.
Fourteen hundred years ago,
Tens of thousands thronged the show,
       In joyous guise,
On the struggle and the strife,
And the pangs of parting life,
       Feasting their eyes.

Then ye might have heard the roar
   Of the noble beasts of prey,
As they fought and bled, before
   Men less noble far than they.
Strength is useless, courage vain,
Beauty saves not—they are slain,
       The forest race;
Whilst the still unsated crowd
For new victims shout aloud,
       To fill their place.

Hark! the Prætor's stern command

Costlier sacrifice proclaims;
Lo! the gladiatorial band,
   Glory of the Roman Games!
As they enter, man by man,
Shape and size the people scan
         With eager glance;
And of each ill-fated pair,
That await the signal there,
         Foretell the chance.

Hark! the trumpet's sudden sound;
   Lo! the work of death begun:
Seas of blood shall drench the ground,
   Ere that deadly work be done.
Ha! a moment of delay?
What the lifted hand can stay?
         Is there a fear
Of Pompeii's fiery shower?
Or, doth Earthquake's giant power
         Make havoc here?

No—for Nature with a smile
   Looks upon her outraged laws,
Man's indignant voice the while
   Bidding man in pity pause.
See!—a monk, obscure, unknown,
Christ's disciple, treads alone
         The arena's sand,
Foe from foe intent to part,
Striving with a zealous heart,
         But feeble hand.

Would ye seek to know his fate?
   Listen to that savage yell!
Scorn, derision, fury, hate,
   Doomed his death—the martyr fell.
Record there is none to show,
Whose the hand that dealt the blow
         That laid him there;
Men who gazed, and men who fought,
All alike to madness wrought,
         The guilt must share.

Whether stoned to death, or slain
  By the sword, or by the spear,
Little recks it—it were vain
  Through the mists of time to peer.
This we know—the martyr died;
Nor without success had plied
          His work of peace,
Since, to expiate that deed,
Rome's Imperial Lord decreed,
          The Games should cease.

Rome obeyed her Lord's commands;
  Never were those Games renewed:
Now the priest of Jesus stands
  Where the gladiator stood.
Thanks, Telemachus, to thee,
Sainted martyr, now we see
          Altars around;
And the spot, where thou of yore
Did'st thy life-blood nobly pour,
          Is hallowed ground.

THE PRUDENT BRIDE.

At Salem Meeting-House, one summer day,
Two lovers, Abby Purkis and John Cole,
Were joined in holy wedlock. Off they started
To spend the honey-moon, gregarious,
At Trenton, Saratoga, and the Falls.
   Reaching this last-named wonder of the world,
They went the usual round; mounted the tower
That overlooks the cataract; stood and watched
The eddying Rapids, and the whirling Pool;
Nor on thy deck, O daring "*Maid of the Mist*,"
Failed they to buffet the tumultuous roar,
The drenching spray, the seeming perilous plunge
Beneath the Horse-Shoe. Every where, throughout,
Abby was brave; nay, on John's stalwart arm
Leaning, was confident.
                   At last they reached
The Cavern of the Winds. Then changed her bearing.
Trembling, she paused. In truth, the howling blasts,
And gusty moans as of imprisoned spirits,
Struck the bride's soul with terror. All aghast,
She stood before the entrance, and refused,
Firmly refused to trust herself within.
John urged—she would not; coaxed—'twas all in vain;
Laughed at, and called her "little fool"—she would not.
Nay more, she prayed him by the love he bore her
Not to set foot himself within a place
So fraught with peril. John was ungallant,
And only laughed the more. Not he the man
To flinch from fisticuffs with Æolus!
Had he not harpooned whales in Arctic seas?
Were not typhoon, white squall, and hurricane
His some time playmates? It was her turn now
To coax, and urge, and crave—and be denied.
   Chafed that her will was not a law to John,
Abby was woman still, and sorely grieved
That he should run such risks. She kissed him fondly,
And bade him tread with care, and hasten back.
Her voice was choked with sobs. Her latest words

Were scarcely audible, though through them breathed
Salem's sound training. "John," she faltered forth,
"We know not what may happen: dear, dear John,
"Were it not well that you—should—leave—with—me—
"Your—watch—and—pocket-book?"

THE TRAMPER'S BED—AND THE KING'S.

Down by the side of a sweet clover-stack,
On a summer night, I lie on my back.
Clear space is above me; and there, as I lie,
I look straight up to the stars in the sky.
   Once, when the King was dethroned by the mob,
They swarmed to his palace, to stare or to rob,
And the frightened lackies flung open the doors,
And clouted shoes scraped along polished floors.
Then it was I caught sight of his Majesty's bed,
With its canopy, gilded and carved, overhead;—
If his Majesty wishes the stars to behold,
And looks up, he can see but the carving and gold!
   Some night, should my soul be unbound as I sleep,
And downward an Angel in search of it sweep,
No bar, no obstruction, would hinder his flight;—
With a wave of his wings, by my corpse he would light.
   But what, if the soul to be loosed were the King's?
Could an Angel reach that by the poise of his wings?
Could he easily cleave through a palace his way?
Through ceilings bedizened, through floors in decay—
Through gorgeous apartments and bare attic rooms,
For lords and for ladies, for valets and grooms—
Through a quaint peakèd roof rising high o'er the whole—
Could he enter, and tenderly waft off the soul?
   Better, then, is the bed by the sweet clover-stack,
With the stars full in view, and the clear Angel's track!
And though much be not mine of this world's pleasant things,
I should care not to barter my couch for the King's!

OCCASION.

From the Italian of Ternaré

"Say, who art thou, with more than mortal air,
Endowed by Heaven with gifts and graces rare,
Whom restless, wingèd feet for ever onward bear?"—

"I am Occasion—known to few, at best;
And since one foot upon a wheel I rest,
Constant my movements are—they cannot be repressed.

"Not the swift eagle in his swiftest flight
Can equal me in speed. My wings are bright;
And man, who sees them waved, is dazzled by the sight.

"My thick and flowing locks, before me thrown,
Conceal my form—nor face, nor breast is shown,
That thus, as I approach, my coming be not known.

"Behind my head, no single lock of hair
Invites the hand, that fain would it grasp there;
But he, who lets me pass, to seize me may despair."

"Whom, then, so close behind thee do I see?"—
"Her name is Penitence; and Heaven's decree
Hath made all those her prey, who profit not by me.

"And thou, O mortal, who dost vainly ply
These curious questions, thou dost not descry,
That now thy time is lost—for I am passing by."

THE MOURNFUL BALLAD OF THE "ALABAMA."

Captain Semmes is on a cruise
O'er the track that skippers use;
From the Western Isles, to those
Near Nantucket shoals, he goes.
                Woe is me, Alabama!

Letters to the merchants tell
Who into his clutches fell;
'Tis the talk of all the town;
News-boys call it up and down
                Woe is me, Alabama!

Straight the sons of Commerce came
To their Chamber, crying shame
For the tidings they had learned,
For their ships and cargoes burned.
                Woe is me, Alabama!

Up and spake a merchant prince:
"Friends, our city well may wince,
For you have, alas! to know
Of a most disastrous blow!
                Woe is me, Alabama!

"All is sunk beneath the waves,
Breadstuffs, lard, tobacco, staves;
Chained have been our Captains bold
In the 'Alabama's' hold!
                Woe is me, Alabama!

"Lawless, too, is Captain Semmes;
Neutral shipments he condemns.
Useless is it to appeal
To Consul's signature and seal.
                Woe is me, Alabama!

"But there's worse than this behind;

Treacherous friends this blow designed.
Great as is the corsair's guilt,
Greater theirs his ship who built!
          Woe is me, Alabama!

"Neutral money, neutral skill,
Wrought us this outrageous ill;
Neutral engines, neutral guns,
Aid him as he fights or runs.
          Woe is me, Alabama!

"Sons of Commerce, men of worth,
Let these words of mine go forth!
Let the British monarch know
That to her all this we owe!"
          Woe is me, Alabama!

So the warning words went forth
To England, from the angered North,
Passed along from mouth to mouth,
"No more dealings with the South!"
          Woe is me, Alabama!

"You may sell to this our land
All we want of contraband;
But have a care that nothing goes,
From you, a neutral, to our foes!"
          Woe is me, Alabama!

Now Heaven preserve us all in peace,
And let these ugly squabbles cease!
So fighters all, and standers-by,
Shall nevermore have cause to cry,
          "Woe is me, Alabama!"

November, 1862.

LINES FOR THE GUITAR.

From the French of Victor Hugo.

Man was saying: "How can we,
In our little boats at sea,
Pass the guarda-costas by?"—
"Row!" said Woman in reply.

Man was saying: "How forget
Perils that our lives beset,
Strife, and Poverty's low cry?"—
"Sleep!" said Woman in reply.

Man was saying: "How be sure
Beauty's favour to secure,
Nor the subtle philtre try?"—
"Love!" said Woman in reply.

THREE MEN AND A WOMAN.

A Summer's dawn and a tranquil sea;
   But lurid all with smoke:
For a bark was burning furiously,
   What time the morning broke.

Terrible? ay, but risk there was none,
   For stern the Captain's sway;
And when he spoke, each mother's son
   Could not but choose obey.

"Man the boats!"—the boats were manned,
   In order, one by one;
To pull a hundred miles to land,
   All under the Summer's sun.

Four stalwart rowers bend to their oars:
   Four sitters at the stern—
Three men and a woman—silent sit,
   Watching the vessel burn.

They were no tremblers: each had known
   Perils by land and deep;
But the woman alone would gently moan,
   And at times, perforce, would weep.

Yet soon the sun was high in heaven,
   And the sea was a-glow: and then
The temper of those men peered out—
   Of those three fearless men.

One thought his white hand by the sun would be tanned;
   One felt they were wrong to risk it,
In sweltering heat, with nothing to eat
   But a bit of dry ship-biscuit.

The third brooded over his handful of freight
   Going down, uninsured, to the deep:
But the woman alone would gently moan,

And at times, perforce, would weep;

Till a sense of shame the three o'ercame,
  And a curious wish to know
Why, still unfearing, she gave way
  To her uncomplaining woe.

"Ah, Sirs!"—she faltered in reply—
  "The danger is easily braved:
But my husband may hear that the ship is burnt—
  And not that we are saved!"

ANOTHER MARBLE FAUN.

A Translation of La Statue, by Victor Hugo.

He seemed to shiver, for the wind was keen.
'Twas a poor statue underneath a mass
Of leafless branches, with a blackened back
And green foot—an old isolated Faun
In old deserted park, who, bending forward,
Half merged himself in the entangled boughs,
Half in his marble settings. He was there,
Pensive, and bound to the earth; and, as all things,
Devoid of movement, he was there—forgotten.

Trees were around him, whipped by the icy blasts—
Gigantic chestnuts, without leaf or bird,
And, like himself, grown old in that same place.
Through the dark network of their undergrowth,
Pallid his aspect; and the earth was brown.
Starless and moonless, a rough winter's night
Was letting down her lappets o'er the mist.
Trees more remote, with sombre shafts upreared,
Each other crossed; and trees remoter still,
By distance blurred, threw up to the grey sky
Their thousand twigs sharp-pointed, intricate;
And posed themselves around; and through the fog
Took, on the horizon's verge, the shadowy form
Of mighty porcupines in countless herd.

This—nothing more: old Faun, dull sky, dark wood.

Piercing the mist, perchance there might be seen
A distant terrace—its long layers of stone
Tinted with slimy green; or group of Nymphs,
Dimly defined beside a wide-spread basin,
And shrinking—fitly in this desolate park—
As once from gazers, from neglect to-day.
The old Faun was laughing. In their dubious haze
Leaving the shamed Nymphs and their dreary basin—
The old Faun was laughing—'twas to him I came
Moved to compassion, for these sculptors all

Are pitiless ever, and, content with praise,
Doom Nymphs to shame, condemn the Fauns to laughter.

   Poor helpless marble, how I've pitied it
Less often man—the harder of the two.
   So then, without a word that might offend
His ear difformed—for well the marble hears
The voice of thought—I said to him: "You hail
From the gay amorous age; O Faun, what saw you,
When you were happy? Were you of the Court?
Did you take part in fêtes?—For your diversion
These Nymphs were fashioned. In this wood, for you,
Capable hands mingled the gods of Greece
With Roman Cæsars; made rare vases peer
Into clear waters; and this garden vext
With tortuous labyrinths. When you were happy,
O Faun, what saw you? All the secrets tell
Of that too vain yet captivating past,
Thick set with prudent love-makers, a past
In which great poets jostled mighty Kings.
How fresh your memory—you are laughing still!

   Speak to me, comely Faun, as you would speak
To tree, or zephyr, or untrodden grass.
From end to end of this well-shaded alley,
When near you, with the handsome Lautrec, passed
The soft-eyed Marguerite, the Bearnaise Queen,
Have you, O Greek, O mocker of old days,
Have you not sometimes with that oblique eye
Winked at the Farnese Hercules?—Alone,
In cave as it were of foliage green and moist,
Have you, O Faun, considerately turned
From side to side when counsel-seekers came,
And now advised as shepherd; now as satyr?
Have you sometimes upon this very bench
Seen at mid-day, Vincent de Paul instilling
Grace into Gondi?—Have you ever thrown
That searching glance on Louis with Fontange,
On Anne with Buckingham; and did they not
Start, with flushed cheeks, to hear your laugh ring forth
From corner of the wood?—Was your advice
As to the thyrsis or the ivy asked,

When, the grand ballet of fantastic form,
God Phœbus, or god Pan, and all his court
Turned the fair head of the fair Montespan,
Calling her Amaryllis?—La Fontaine,
Flying the courtiers' ears of stone, came he,
Tears in his eyelids, to reveal to you
The sorrows of his Nymphs of Vaux?—What said
Boileau to you, to you, O lettered Faun,
Who once with Virgil, in the Eclogue, held
That charming dialogue, and deftly made—
Couched on the turf—the heavy spondee dance
To the light dactyl's step?—Say, have you seen
Young beauties sporting on the sward: Chevreuse
Of the swimming eyes, Thiange of airs superb?
Have they sometimes, in rosy-tinted group,
Girt you so fondly round, that all at once
A straggling sunbeam on a fluttering bosom
Marked your lascivious profile?—Has your tree
Received beneath the quiet of its shade
Pale Mazarin's scarlet winding sheet?—Have you
Been honoured with a sight of Molière
In dreamy mood? Has he perchance at times,
Dropping at random a melodious verse,
In tone familiar—as is the wont
'Twixt demi-gods—addressed you?—When at eve
Homeward hereby the thinker went, has he
Who—seeing souls all naked—could not fear
Your nudity, in his enquiring mind
Confronted you with Man? And did he deem
You, spectral cynic, the less sad, less cold,
Less wicked, less ironical—comparing
Your laugh in marble with our human laugh?"

    Under the thickly tangled branches, thus
Did I speak to him; he no answer gave—
Not even a murmur. On the pedestal
Leaning, I listened; but the past stirred not.
Dumb to my words and to my pity deaf,
The Satyr, motionless, was vaguely blanched
By the wan glimmer of the dying day.
To see him there, sinister, half drawn out
From his dark framing, and by damp discoloured,

Brought to one's mind the handle of a sword
In torso chiselled—an old rusty sword,
Left for long years neglected in its sheath.

I shook my head, and moved myself away.
Then, from the copses, from the dried up boughs
Pendent above him, from secret caves
Hid in the wood, methought a ghostly voice
Came forth and woke an echo in my soul,
As in the hollow of an amphora.

"Imprudent poet," thus it seemed to say,
"What dost thou here? Leave the forsaken Fauns
In peace beneath their trees! Dost thou not know,
Poet, that ever it is impious deemed,
In desert spots where drowsy shades repose—
Though love itself might prompt thee—to shake down
The moss that hangs from ruined centuries,
And, with the vain noise of thine ill-timed words,
To mar the recollections of the dead?"

Then to the gardens all enwrapped in mist
I hurried, dreaming of the vanished days.
And still the tree-tops were with mystery rife;
And still, behind me—hieroglyph obscure
Of antique alphabet—the lonely Faun
Held to his laughter, through the falling night.

I went my way; but yet—in saddened spirit
Pondering on all that had my vision crossed,
Floating in air or scattered under foot,
Confused and blent, beauty and spring and morn,
Leaves of old summers, fair ones of old time—
Through all, at distance would my fancy see,
In the woods, statues; shadows in the past!

CHARADES.

I.

Look from the prow of thine anchored bark—
Anchored by classic shore—and mark,
Down fathoms-deep in the purple sea,
How Time and the waters have dealt on me

Art lost in the moonless and starless night?
Far-away looming, a light! a light!
Fearlessly steer, for on me 'tis placed,
To guide thy bark o'er the trackless waste

Earth knows me, too; and will heave and quake
Where my subterranean course I take:
And none so aghast at my ravages then,
As they whose type was the Sire of men.

But not ever thus; at times I'm seen
On the cheek or the neck of Beauty's queen;
Or (to favoured mortal alone confest)
Tinging the snow upon Beauty's breast.

So, whether above the waves, or below,
Or beneath the Earth, or on breast of snow,
Linked with the past, or alive to-day,
Tell who I am—if tell ye may.

II.

My lady calls; my First obeys—
   Nor less his lord's behest:
In bower and hall, in olden days,
   My First was in request.

Yet 'tis my First that tells us now
   What then my First was doing;
How he went forth to war, and how
   He prospered in his wooing.

A wise King bade the lazy fool

Observe my Second's ways,
And notice—as it were in school—
    The wisdom she displays.

Yet hers is a devouring race,
    And might—though strange it be—
Eat up, in given time and place,
    My First, or you, or me.

As for my whole—in every age
    Mankind must have its show;
In actual life, on mimic stage,
    In peace, war, joy, or woe.

Now 'tis a wedding, now a death,
    A gathering, or a play;
It comes, but, like a passing breath,
    Full soon 'tis swept away.

III.

When Richard of the Lion Heart
    In arms the Paynim sought,
I of his panoply was part,
    And, wielding me, he fought.

When ladies on a different field
    With men their skill essay,
I am the weapon that they wield
    If they would gain the day.

When cooks in certain dishes show
    Their culinary art,
I am on hand—the masters know
    What flavour I impart.

IV.

I'm a word of one syllable. Look you for me
Mid Niagara's roar; in the turbulent sea;
Where the winds and the waters are wildest at play,
And fling off their laughter in volumes of spray.

I'm a noun of five letters; but throw one aside—

I'm a verb; with the noun I'm no longer allied.
I'm a grave, solemn verb; nay, I truly might say,
Those who follow my precept do nothing but pray.

But again; let two letters be dropped—there's a change;
As a noun—and by no means a grave one—I range.
Now I'm here; now I'm there; seen by night and by day,
For in short, I'm a beam, or a flash, or a ray.

Thus a verb and two nouns packed together you see,
In a word of one syllable.—What can it be?

V.

There are some words, that in a double sense
Must be interpreted; of these am I.
Your housemaid, thus, wilt know me literally
Better than you do; but, with all respect
For Betty's carefulness, she scarce can catch
My finer meaning. I'm, with her, a thing
For brush and duster; in me, you behold
A symbol. So much for me as I stand.
Now cut my head off—I'm another word
Of narrow and of wide significance,
Handful of dust, the very world itself.
Cut off my tail—the effect is still the same;
I'm yet another of those duplex words:
Mental and bodily, an essential part
Of all mankind, without which no one lives,
Nay, not an animal, though you may swear,
And truly too, that I have no existence,
And never had, in certain men and women.
     Enough: it is not difficult to find
Three words, six meanings, in one syllable.

VI.

Well may I call myself cosmopolite,
Being of all lands and times. Barbaric tribes
Know me, and honour. In the gentler world,
Scholars have studied me, and poets sung,
And painters painted, and musicians hymned.
Nor from Religion have I held myself
Apart. In Pagan and in savage rites

Largely I mingle; and some Saints at least,
Worshipped among us, owe me much. In short,
Theme, inspiration, puzzle—I am all.
As to my form, it may not be defined;
Yet this is certain: were I rent in twain
And of one half bereft, I should not have
A leg to stand on—of the other half
Equally mulcted, I should endless be.

VII.

In me, as the scholar saith,
Is exhaustion, wasting, death.
But—so close do grave and gay
Touch, in this our world—you may,
By a change of accent made,
Change the meaning I conveyed;
Change me so that I proclaim
Victory won, and spoils, and fame!

VIII.

My first's a French noun; and, without it, stands not
Church, palace, or hospital, villa, or cot.
My Second no feature distinctive can claim;
It but echoes my First—'t is precisely the same.
   Yet my Whole to French parentage makes no pretence;
It is plain Anglo-Saxon, in sound as in sense;
Nor more widely asunder does pole lie from pole,
Than my Gallican parts and my Anglican whole.
Impalpable, it—solid, tangible, they;
They may last, for long ages—it passes away!
Now a sign of approval, a token of scorn;
Sometimes of the wind or the waves it is born;
Though its presence at intervals surely you'll trace
Where my First and my Second have stablished their place;
Where King hath his dwelling or Trade hath her marts—
A whole evanescent, material parts!